The Ghost Squad
and the
Prowling Hermits

The Ghost Squad and the Prowling Hermits

by E. W. Hildick

 A Ghost Squad Book

E. P. DUTTON   NEW YORK

LIBRARY OF CONGRESS CATALOGING IN PUBLICATION DATA

Hildick, E. W. (Edmund Wallace), date
   The Ghost Squad and the prowling hermits.

   (A Ghost Squad book)
   Summary: The members of the Ghost Squad determine to
keep the evil Dr. Purcell from succeeding in his plan to
have his ghostly accomplices take over the temporarily
vacated bodies of living beings.
   [1. Ghosts—Fiction.   2. Mystery and detective stories]
I. Title.   II. Series: Hildick, E. W. (Edmund Wallace),
date.   Ghost Squad book.
PZ7.H5463Ggg   1987   [Fic]   87-8889
ISBN 0-525-44330-4

Published in the United States by E. P. Dutton,
2 Park Avenue, New York, N.Y. 10016,
a division of NAL Penguin Inc.

Published simultaneously in Canada by
Fitzhenry & Whiteside Limited, Toronto

Editor: Ann Durell

Printed in the U.S.A.   COBE   First Edition
10 9 8 7 6 5 4 3 2 1

To Maureen and Don Bakewell
and all the others at Mayroyd
who provided this hermit with a
delightful and much needed haven

Contents

The Ghost Squad
and the
Prowling Hermits

1
Barefoot in the Snow

"Hey, Karen! Isn't that Sylvia Green? Danny's sister?"

"Where?"

"Over there. At the edge of the crowd. The little kid in the—the—"

"In the yellow pajamas! Gosh, yes!"

Both Carlos Gomez and Karen Hansen were now staring across the street with great concern. And no wonder. For although the sun was shining on the crowd outside Dino's Discounts store, it was also shining on fresh snow, creating sparkling points of emerald and orange and pink. There was a chill breeze. Almost everyone else in the crowd was bundled up as they awaited the arrival heralded on the banner above the store:

SANTA HERE 11 A.M.
SATURDAY, DECEMBER 15

It was nearly 11:30. Loudspeakers had just started to boom out "I'm Dreaming of a White Christmas" for the sixth or seventh time. Dino Gorusso gave his Giants cap a tug as he glared out of an upper window, champing on the end of a dead cigar.

"Sure wouldn't like to be in that Santa's boots when Dino gets ahold of him!" said one elderly bystander.

"At least his feet'll be warm," grumbled his companion.

The younger members of the crowd didn't seem to mind the cold. Some of the little kids were already being held up by their parents, staring at the rooftops as if expecting the visitor to drop from the sky. Many of the older kids were throwing snowballs.

Sylvia Green, a tiny pale-faced five-year-old who looked more like three, had no young companions to pass the time with, however—nor any adult to lift her up. She was simply drifting about on the fringe of the crowd with a bewildered expression, her eyes as glazed as those of the grubby pink teddy bear she was clutching.

"He isn't here yet!" she said to the bear. "Just be quiet, or I'll take you home!"

The bear hadn't said a word, of course. And it was as if Sylvia hadn't spoken, either, for all the attention the people nearby paid her. None of *them* seemed bothered about the way she was dressed, or the fact that her feet were bare.

4

Only Karen and Carlos were showing any concern—and that concern was deepening.

"What's she doing dressed like *that?*" said Karen, in a hushed tone.

Carlos gulped.

"I heard Danny say she's been sick. Flu or something. Maybe she got bored, lying in bed. Uh—maybe she snuck out."

He didn't sound very convinced. Neither did Karen, when she replied.

"But how come she was *able* to sneak out? What about her mother?"

"Oh—*her!*" said Carlos.

Karen nodded. They both knew about Mrs. Green.

"Still, you'd think one of the others would keep an eye on her. Mike or Jilly. They—"

Karen was interrupted by a shout from the crowd and an abrupt switch of tune. Now it was "Jingle Bells" as, slowly, on the back of a truck made up to look like a sleigh, the hero of the hour appeared, farther up the street.

"Stay where y'are!" bellowed Dino, flinging open the window as some of the kids ran toward the truck. "Make way for Santa Claus!" he boomed, more jovially. "The bum!" he added in a low growl, glancing at his watch.

It was already 11:35.

As Santa stepped down, uneasy in his boots and wheezing under the weight of his sack, the crowd began to cluster around. Little kids in their parents' arms were reaching out to touch him. One made a grab for

5

his beard. An older kid, a boy, stared hard at his nose and eyes, then leered and said, "Hey! I recognize him! It's only Tommy—"

"Stand back!" growled Dino Gorusso, steering the boy aside. Then: "Welcome, Santa Claus!" he intoned, putting an arm around the crimson-cloaked shoulders. "Welcome! Welcome! Welcome!"

With each "Welcome!" Dino gave a squeeze that made the guest of honor wince.

"Your Fairy Grotto is all ready and waiting for ya. Where the kids can come and tell you what they want for Christmas. Why—" Dino added, grinning benignly but giving an extra-vicious squeeze, "I guess I'll be talking to ya myself, later!"

As the guest was led to the door, the crowd surged forward. Sylvia began trying to find a way to the front, frantically tapping the backs of those nearest to her.

"Oh, boy!" groaned Carlos. "I don't like the way nobody seems to feel anything when she touches them!"

"Me either!" said Karen. "Come on!"

They hurried across. They left no prints in the piled-up snow at the curbs, but no one noticed this. None of the people they brushed past even noticed *them*— and this too was strange. After all, neither Karen nor Carlos was dressed for that temperature any better than Sylvia. Carlos was wearing a T-shirt and jeans, and Karen had on a flimsy red shirt and white shorts.

But they weren't in the least bothered by this lack of attention. They were used to it. What did bother them was the fact that the little girl herself obviously *could* see them, as they approached.

"Hi!" she said, looking up at Karen. "Will you lift me up, please? I wanna see Santa."

"Oh, no!" Carlos softly groaned. "This definitely means she must have—"

Karen nudged him as she stooped to pick up Sylvia. She knew only too well that Carlos's next words were likely to be: "This definitely means she must have died! She must be like us. A ghost herself!"

2
Hermit on the Prowl

"Not necessarily," said Karen as she lifted Sylvia.

"No, I guess not!" grunted Carlos.

"Gee, thanks!" said Sylvia. She hadn't been listening to the other two. She'd been far too busy staring over the heads of the crowd. "Santa! Hi, Santa!"

None of those heads turned at the sound of her shrill voice. Only ghosts can hear—or see, or feel—other ghosts. But Sylvia wasn't of the same kind as her two helpers.

"I guess she's just a temporary," said Carlos. "An *astral* body. Probably took off when her physical body got delirious."

"Of course," said Karen. "It has to be that. She was still alive yesterday, according to Danny. And you know as well as I do how long it takes for a ghost to return after someone has really died."

"All right, all right!"

Carlos was feeling sore. *Sure* he knew it usually takes about four months. After all, although he was only thirteen and Karen was sixteen, he'd been a ghost for nearly as long as the girl. And wasn't he the scientific brains of the group that called themselves the Ghost Squad? Why, after the Halloween Conspiracy case, he'd solemnly declared in front of the others that "from now on, I, Carlos Gomez, will be taking a very special interest in any temporary ghosts we come across."

"Anyway," he said, "we'd better get her back to her real body or she might easily *become* a permanent ghost."

"You're right," Karen said, beginning to turn away.

"Santa! Santa!" yelled Sylvia, tugging at Karen's long blond hair. "Take me to him! Please!"

Karen winced. Ghosts couldn't directly hurt living people no matter how hard they tried, but they could certainly make other ghosts feel pain!

"We have to take you home, honey," she said.

"No! No! No! I wanna see Santa. . . . *Teddy* wants to see Santa!"

"Teddy wants to go home."

"No! *No!* NO!"

Sylvia's screams got louder. Still they didn't attract the attention of most of those gathered around the door, where Dino was trying to persuade Santa to say a few general words to the public.

But Sylvia's ghost hadn't been the only one wanting to get near Santa. A man in a fur hat and a long leather raincoat had also been hovering around. And, as the screaming kid was carried past him, he turned and scrutinized her closely. His heavy-lidded eyes narrowed, and his loose red lips tightened into a thoughtful fleshy bunch.

"Uh-oh!" murmured Carlos.

"What?"

"Don't look now, but I think we're being followed."

"Santa! Santa!" yelled Sylvia.

"Followed?" said Karen.

"Yeah. Big guy. Youngish, with a fat face and mustache and long leather coat. Nasty oily eyes."

"You sure?"

"Positive. It was Sylvia who attracted his attention."

"Don't wanna go home!" yelled Sylvia.

"Malev?" asked Karen, mentioning their name for the hating type of ghost—the kind feared by other ghosts as being highly dangerous.

"Definitely."

"And you say he's interested in Sylvia?" said Karen, risking a quick backward look as they turned a corner.

The man was plodding along about twenty yards behind—close enough for Karen to notice *he* was leaving no footprints, either.

She quickened her pace.

"Come on. We'll have to give him the slip. Looks like he could have been a child molester when he was alive."

"Looks worse to me."

"Worse?"

10

"Yeah." Carlos's frown deepened. "He could be a Hermit."

"A *Hermit?*" Karen's voice rose into a squeak. "You mean a Hermit-type ghost?"

"What else?"

This was also a name known to most ghosts. It came from the hermit crab, the creature that has no shell of its own, but prowls around looking for shells vacated by other creatures—dead snails and so on. Except that *dead* human bodies were no use to Hermit ghosts. The bodies had to be still alive—simply vacated temporarily. The bodies of people who were drugged, or drunk, or so mad that they were "beside themselves" with rage—anyone whose built-in ghost, whose "astral body," had gone for a walk.

Including people who were delirious.

"You think he's guessed she's only a temporary?" said Karen.

She glanced at the little girl. The kid seemed to be getting drowsy.

"Yeah," said Carlos. "He's hoping we'll lead him to where her real body is. Then he'll hope to get in first."

Karen shuddered. She knew that ghosts who took over a vacated body never lasted long. They soon burned out. But to make sure of that vacancy they usually killed the wandering temporary ghost first. And ghosts *could* kill other ghosts.

"We'd better lose him," said Karen. "He obviously doesn't know where she lives."

"That could take too much time," said Carlos. "Sylvia's physical body must be in a coma. The longer she vacates it, the more dangerous it will be for her, Hermit or no Hermit."

"But—"

"Listen. I have a better idea. You go on ahead, straight to her home, and *I'll* keep him busy."

"But, Carlos—"

"Go on! You're the champion runner! As soon as you turn the next corner, *move!* I'll be OK."

3
In the
Malev's Grip

None of the regular living passersby near the corner of Railroad Street could see what happened next, of course. If they had, they would certainly have stopped to witness the encounter between Carlos Gomez and the Hermit.

"Sir! Just a second!"

Carlos looked very small as he stepped in front of the other, who'd just started to put on speed when Karen and Sylvia had turned the corner.

"Outa my way, kid!"

The big man had a strangely light husky voice. But it had a menacing grate in it. He was at least six feet tall, and he looked even taller and bulkier in the high fur hat and heavy leather raincoat.

"But it's very important, sir!"

Carlos often had a sharp urgent look. His eyes, under the shaggy dark hair, were quick and bright and watchful, like those of a busy sheepdog. Right now, his expression was more intensely urgent than ever.

"What is it, then?"

The man had pushed him to one side at the corner, but had then paused, now that he was able to see Karen and Sylvia in the distance.

Carlos's sharp eyes noted this. He frowned. He'd been hoping that Karen would have had time to turn into the street where Sylvia lived, just beyond the pool hall. Probably the extra burden had slowed her down.

"Well?"

The husky growl reminded him of his own part of the mission.

"I—I think you dropped something. Just back there, around the corner."

"Huh?"

The man turned, took a couple of steps—then swung around.

"*Hey!*" The sloppy red lips had started to curl. "What *is* this?" The man grabbed a handful of Carlos's shirt, just above the printed logo: the large *G* with the letters of the alphabet and other symbols grouped around it at the ends of spokes. "*You* know we don't have things to drop!"

Carlos tried to wriggle free.

"I—I forgot. . . ."

He knew very well that all the clothes worn by a ghost, or anything a ghost might be carrying, were really part of the total ghost personality. The clothes

14

were usually those which a ghost had felt best in around the time of death—and any objects carried, like Sylvia's toy bear, were part of that chosen outfit, fused to the ghost body as firmly as if it were an extra limb. It would have been as impossible for a ghost to drop something as it would have been to drop the hand that carried it.

He glanced along Railroad Street and was glad to note that Karen and Sylvia were no longer in view.

"Don't lie to me, you little jerk!"

The Malev was furious. His grip tightened. He may have looked flabby, but there was nothing weak about the muscles of his right hand.

"Sir—I—"

"You were with those other two. You're deliberately stalling me, aren't you?"

He brought his face down close to Carlos's. The hatred that blazed from under the heavy dark lids seemed also to have tightened up the sloppiness of his mouth. His appearance became even worse as he allowed a grin to spread, showing a set of yellow teeth with a single unnaturally white one gleaming just right of the central upper pair.

Carlos stared at the white tooth as the man said slowly, "But there's one thing a ghost can drop!"

"Sir?"

"Yeah! *Another* ghost!"

Suddenly, Carlos felt the world spin as he was lifted bodily, choking on the tightened folds of his shirt. Then, with a frighteningly easy twist of the man's arm, he was turned upside down.

15

"So how would it be if I dropped *you?*"

Carlos began to kick. The man held him at arm's length.

"Let me go!"

Dropping wouldn't cause a problem, Carlos knew. Neither the packed snow nor the bare patch of concrete a few feet farther along would make any impression on *his* head—no matter from what height he was dropped.

The other seemed to remember this, too.

He swung Carlos back on his feet. But the evil leer was still spread, the white tooth was still gleaming and, worst of all, the grip was still tight.

"But I'm not going to drop you. What I do aim to do"—the leer became a snarl—"is to choke the day-lights outa you, instead!"

His left hand shot up and gripped Carlos by the throat.

Carlos felt his eyes bulge.

"Ga—ga—!" he choked.

This was something else. Something *really* deadly. A ghost's hand, or foot, if strong enough, could do just as much damage to another ghost's body as if both had been made of living tissue. Slapping, clawing, gouging, punching, chopping, choking, kicking, stomping—just as in life, some of these could be lethal.

Especially choking . . .

Detective Grogan strolled by, his eyes alert for Christmas pickpockets. He almost walked through Carlos's assailant, but the Malev stepped aside. Carlos

16

rolled his eyes in abguish. The sensation a living body made when it went through a ghost wasn't exactly devastating—simply a rather sickening wave of warmth. But it might just have been strong enough to startle the Malev and loosen his grip.

Anyway, it didn't seem to be Carlos's day. As the cop went on, without the slightest suspicion that a major felony was being perpetrated literally under his nose, the boy knew he'd just have to rely on his own rapidly dwindling resources.

He reached up and tried to pry open the cruel fingers.

It only made things worse. He felt as if a dark red cloud were starting to engulf him, making his ears buzz.

"Don't worry," he heard the man say as the grip was relaxed a little. "I don't aim to crush your windpipe—yet."

"I—gug! Please—"

Lightning flashes of excruciating pain were beginning to shoot through and out of that red cloud in all directions.

"I don't aim to do it at *all*. So long as you tell me where that kid lives."

The red cloud was lifting. The pain subsided. Carlos stared at the evil eager face.

"Who—uh—what kid?"

Out of the corners of his eyes, Carlos spotted Karen again, still with Sylvia in her arms, returning. Luckily, the Malev had his back to them. Carlos wondered why Karen was acting so dumb. He flung out an arm, trying to wave his friend back, hoping the Malev himself wouldn't turn and spot them.

"*You* know what kid! The one your girlfriend was carrying."

"I don't know what you're talking about!"

"Oh, no? Then we'll have to see what a little more gentle persuasion will—"

"*Stop that, Maggot! You fool!*"

Even as the Malev's grip began to tighten again, the crisp command rang out, somewhere behind Carlos—and a look of most abject terror swept across that flabby face.

Quickly, the grip was relaxed.

"Release him, oaf! Immediately!"

Rubbing his neck, Carlos turned to see who could have made such an electrifying impression on his assailant.

4
Dr. Purcell— and Company

At first, Carlos wasn't sure. Two men were approaching. Both were staring straight at the Malev.

One was as big as Maggot, but his face was smooth and impassive, and he walked slightly behind the other. And, yes, the man in the lead was definitely the one who'd rapped out the command. He was the one Maggot seemed to be looking at as he mumbled, "But— but, Dr. Purcell—"

"Is *this* what you were detailed to do? Did I ask you to wander around brawling, like the lout you obviously still are?"

The voice was the same: not loud, but crisp, dry, carrying, commanding. Carlos studied the man.

He was slightly built. Maggot could have made two of him. Nor was there anything immediately striking about the doctor's dress: just a thick gray green tweed suit with a white shirt and dark necktie. He wore heavy-soled brown lace-up shoes and was bareheaded. But even Carlos, who was no connoisseur of fashion, could tell that the suit fit beautifully, and that the thick gray brown hair had been cut by an artist. Dr. Purcell wasn't as suitably dressed for the snow as Maggot, yet he didn't seem at all out of place. Carlos couldn't be sure whether this meant the man must have died sometime one late fall or early spring, and he was equally undecided about the man's age. At a distance of a few yards, the newcomer had looked quite young, but now that Dr. Purcell was up close, Carlos was shocked to see how wrinkled that face was. Finely wrinkled, puckered and pouched like a lizard's—with a vicious snapping slit of a mouth and a sour, severe, cold expression.

Carlos shuddered, glad that those pale gray eyes weren't fixed on him.

"But they were leading me to a *vacancy!*" whined Maggot. "Look! The kid in pajamas, Dr. Purcell! That one!"

Karen had stopped, farther along. Sylvia still seemed to be in a daze as Karen hugged her closer.

Dr. Purcell gave the two girls a swift disdainful glance, then turned back.

"How many more times must I tell you, idiot? There must be optimum compatibility for a Hermit to survive in another body. At least ten different crucial points." He turned and gave Sylvia another glance. "And between you and her there isn't even one. Not in sex, nor size, nor coloring, nor—" The slit mouth snapped shut. Then: "Ah, but why should I go through them all yet again, Muscle?" he said, addressing the other man. "Maggot is so—*you* tell him!"

The impassive face brightened—but not with any friendly expression. "St-stupid!"

The Malev called Muscle seemed to twitch all over as he bent his dark glasses toward Maggot. Now *he* had definitely died one warm summer's day, Carlos decided. His face was deeply tanned, and he wore a white jacket and white slacks with a black open-necked shirt. A golden crucifix glistened in a nest of dark chest hairs. His hair was black, and he looked a dashing vigorous twenty-five or twenty-six. And he'd certainly been well named. Carlos watched those suddenly twitching muscles—the big ones bulging under the shoulder pads of the jacket, the small knotted ones at the sides of the mouth and around the neck. They twitched even more as he continued to address Maggot.

"A dumb, st-stupid jerk, arguing with the doc! Sh-shall I w-waste him, sir?" he asked. "Sh-shall I j-just t-take him out and—and—" He seemed to be stuttering not because of any physical impediment, but because it made him seethe with indignation and rage every time he turned those opaque black lenses on Maggot.

Maggot seemed to have shrunk a good twelve inches. He was trembling violently. Dr. Purcell held out a restraining arm.

"Calm down, Muscle! Let us at least see if the mooncalf is capable of learning from his mistakes." He turned to Maggot. Ghosts might not be able to feel the normal cold, Carlos reflected—but those eyes of Dr. Purcell had a windchill factor all their own. Maggot's trembling ceased as if he'd been instantaneously freeze-dried. "You were sent to study someone who *is* compatible with you. In age, in—"

"Yeah!" bleated Maggot. "But he wasn't drunk, just a little unsteady—"

"I know *that*, half-wit! At this time of day, even he can't have drunk himself into anything like a—uh—suitable donor state. But you were sent to familiarize yourself with him—his mannerisms, his gait, his attitude toward others when reasonably sober—*not* to take him over!"

"Yes—yes, sir! But when I see this kid, wandering out of a living body, which you can always tell on account of the pajamas—"

"Exactly! You were a cheap opportunist in life, Maggot, and it seems that you'll never shake off your old habits. Now listen." There was something very vicious in the way that slit mouth seemed to bite on the words, snapping and clipping and spitting out the bits. "I've told you once and I will tell you one more time only. There is a complete lack of compatibility between you and that child. If you *had* taken over her body, do you know how long you'd have lasted? Eh? Hmm? Eh?"

Maggot dropped his thick-lidded eyes.

"Well—uh—"

"Thirty seconds. Thir-ty sec-onds. Maximum . . ."

Suddenly Dr. Purcell seemed to become aware of the audience.

"Well?" he said, turning that freezing stare onto Carlos. "What are you gaping at, lad? You—and your little friend"—Karen shrank as the stare was switched to Sylvia—"both had a lucky escape, that's all."

"Yes, sir," said Carlos, beginning to move away. "Thanks!"

"*Wait!*"

The command rang out angrily. And once again the doctor's anger seemed to trigger a much more violent and volcanic anger in Muscle.

"The doc s-says to—to w-wait!"

The white-clad arm had shot out in front of Carlos.

"Sure!" Carlos wasn't about to argue with that arm. He turned. "Sir?"

"This child," said Dr. Purcell. "I take it she *is* in a temporary state of ghosthood?"

"Yes, sir. It's her astral body, all right," said Carlos.

Dr. Purcell raised his shreddy eyebrows.

" 'Astral body,' eh? You seem to be familiar with the terminology. Tell me more. In this child's case, what caused it to walk? Night terrors? Sickness?"

"Oh, sickness!" said Carlos. "Yes, sir. Delirium. We—we think."

The ghost of a ghost of a smile flitted across the network of wrinkles, causing a pucker to swell here and a pouch to deflate elsewhere.

"Well, I'm sure it wasn't drink or drugs in *her* case!"

Karen spoke up. "She—her living body has flu."

"So the child *isn't* in the habit of doing this?" Dr. Purcell said, continuing to scrutinize Carlos.

"No, sir!" said Karen, her eyes flashing at being so coldly ignored. Then she frowned. "In—in the habit?"

The man nodded, still looking at Carlos.

"He means like Buzz Phillips," explained Carlos. "When he dreams, he can see himself sleeping." Carlos turned back to the doctor. "That's when *his* astral body sometimes takes a walk, sir. Not far, but—"

"Exactly." The man frowned thoughtfully. "Uh—this Buzz Phillips. Is he a friend of yours?"

"Yes." This time, Carlos left off the *sir*, suddenly uneasy.

"And he is still alive?"

"Sure."

"Interesting." Even as he said the word, the man seemed to lose interest. "Anyway, you'd better run along and get that child back into her physical body. Judging from the look of her, I should say you haven't much time."

Sylvia was still looking glazed. Karen gave the small body an extra hitch.

"Yes, come on," she said.

As they walked away, Karen said, "What did you tell him *that* for?"

"What?" mumbled Carlos, knowing very well what. "About Buzz."

"Well—uh—why not? I mean the guy seemed interested. And—and after all, he did help us."

24

"Yes," said Karen. "But what was it all about? It seems like some regular gang's at work."

"I know. And that's another reason I wanted to keep him talking. To find out as much as we could. I mean—well—this could turn out to be another major case for the Ghost Squad."

Karen didn't argue with that. She'd been thinking exactly the same herself.

5
Sylvia's Homecoming

"Anyway," said Carlos, "you heard what he said. We need to get Sylvia back to her body first." He frowned. "By the way, what made you come back?"

"Because when I got there, the street door was closed and the house looked deserted," said Karen. "Are you sure Danny didn't say she was in the hospital?"

"Danny," murmured Sylvia, blinking at Carlos with a look of faint perplexity.

"Positive!" said Carlos. "He said he'd been to look in at the house. He said he was worried to see how sick Sylvia looked, but pleased at the way his mother was shaping up."

They were silent for a while as they hurried along. A snowball aimed at a living girl by a living boy went straight through the *G* on Carlos's chest and out between his shoulder blades. He hardly noticed, so busy was he, thinking about the Green household. While Danny was alive, Mrs. Green had been a very negligent mother—partly because of the struggle to raise five kids on her earnings as a cleaning woman, and partly because of her drinking problem. When Danny had been killed, everyone thought her drinking would increase. But the accident seemed to have shaken her up in a constructive way. And when she started to collect the compensation money, things began to get better all around for the surviving kids. At least they were getting enough to eat now, Carlos reflected, looking at Sylvia's deathly white but chubby face.

"Mrs. Green must still be very sloppy, though," said Karen, who'd obviously been following a similar line of thought. "I mean she should have had the sense to get Sylvia into the hospital days ago."

"Well . . . maybe she has by now."

"But that's just what I'm worried about! Where to take her before it's too late!" Karen gave Sylvia a pecking kiss. "Honey—listen. Where were you? Before you went to see Santa."

Sylvia blinked.

"Bed."

"Sure! But which bed?"

"Bed," Sylvia murmured again, her eyelids drooping.

"Oh, boy!" groaned Karen. "Look, Carlos—we know what happens when a ghost falls asleep, don't we?"

"Sure. We just disappear for a day or two."

"So is that what happens to a temporary ghost?"

Carlos shrugged.

"I don't know. I've never—"

"Because if it does, and this—Sylvia's astral body—disappears for a day or two, it really will be too late."

"Maybe. I—anyway, there's Mike and Jilly. Let's catch up and go into the house with them."

Mike and Jilly were Sylvia's brother and sister. Mike was ten and Jilly had just made nine—but, like Sylvia, they looked small for their ages, despite their huge brand-new purple quilted jackets. They had just come out of the nearby pharmacy and were barreling along like a couple of purple balloons driven by the wind.

"Mike! Jilly!" cried Sylvia.

Naturally, the two kids didn't hear her.

"Hey! Mike! *Jilly!*" They were only a couple of steps ahead. Sylvia sobbed—then screamed, "You *never* wait for me!"

Still no response. Sylvia raised the toy bear, ready to hit her sister with it as they all turned the corner by the pool hall.

"I'll tell Momma!" Sylvia screamed, taking a swipe at Jilly and missing.

They were at the door of the house now. Mike was turning the handle. As soon as the door opened, Jilly darted in. Mike wasn't slow to follow, but by the time he closed the door, the other three were in the dark hall too.

"That you, Mike? Jilly?"

The hoarse voice came from somewhere at the end of the hall.

"Yes, Mom," said Jilly, bursting into a room there.

"Well, hurry, hurry!" screeched the voice. Then it flattened into a wail. "I think she's going! Your little sister is going!"

They followed Mike into the room. It was chaotic, but that was mainly because it had been turned into a sickroom, with most of the furniture pushed to one side to make room for a bed. The heavy figure of Mrs. Green, shaking with sobs, was bending over what looked like a bundle of yellow clothes. Another child, as small as Sylvia—her brother Arnie—was tugging at his mother's sleeve and bawling hysterically.

"Oh, no!" cried Mike, reaching the bedside.

"No! Please! Please, no!" sobbed Jilly, trying to elbow him aside.

Sylvia wriggled out of Karen's arms and ran forward, crying out, "Momma!"

Then she stopped at the edge of the bed, suddenly silent, staring down at her own body.

"What now?" whispered Karen. "Is—is she dead?"

Carlos frowned.

"Hard to tell."

The child on the bed was very, very still. Her hair was spiky with sweat. Her eyes were closed, but a bead of moisture was slowly trickling from the corner of her right eye. The bear—the real pink toy bear— was still being tightly clutched in one outflung hand.

Her astral body stared at the real bear, then at its

replica, then at the motionless sweat-soaked face. Then, with a deep sigh, it swayed forward, rolling as it went, and lay on top of the other, assuming exactly the same position right down to the outflung bear, before suddenly—with no movement of the bedclothes that even the two watching ghosts could detect—disappearing.

Jilly's cry cut through the sobs and wailing.

"Her eyes are opening!"

Mrs. Green stiffened.

"You're right! You're right! *Oh, my baby!*"

Sylvia was looking up and around, blinking, a faint smile hovering on her lips.

"Momma!" she whispered, in a croaky voice.

"My baby!"

"Is she gonna be OK, Mom?" Mike whispered.

"I—I think so!" said Mrs. Green. "The fever must have broke. . . . Sylvia, Sylvia—can you see me?"

"Sure! . . . Why are you crying, Mom?"

The little girl's voice was still croaky. But it was getting firmer.

"Hush, honey!" said Mrs. Green. "You've been very sick, but now—now you'll be just fine."

Sylvia slowly looked around. "Hi, Jilly! Hi, Mike!" The bright eyes traveled on, seeming to meet Karen's and Carlos's but never pausing. "Hi, Arnie!" She turned back to her mother. "I been dreaming, Momma. Guess what? Mike, Jilly—big smart Jilly—I bet *you* can't guess!"

"Hush! Rest!" said Mrs. Green. "You can tell us later."

30

"No! Wanna tell you now. I dreamed I saw *Santa!*"
Arnie stared.

"Did you get to talk to him? Did you tell him I wanted a—?"

"No. But I went real close to him. There was an angel, too."

"Angel, honey?" said Mrs. Green, crossing herself.

"Yeah. She carried me. A beautiful lady with long yellow hair. And white—white—"

"White robe?" suggested Jilly.

"Naw! Kinda like shorts. With a red shirt—red like *Santa's* robe. And—and there was this devil boy, only he wasn't really bad, he was her friend, only *he* wasn't beautiful."

Karen had blushed at Sylvia's description of her. Carlos had started to smile, but now the smile had turned sour.

"OK, Angel Lady!" he said, giving Karen an unnecessarily sharp nudge. "Let's get ready to leave. We have work to do, remember—and Mike looks like he's going out again."

Mrs. Green had noticed this, too.

"Where are you going, Mike? I—"

"Just to tell Mr. Clark at the pharmacy. We promised to let him know if anything happened, good or bad."

"I know someone else who'll be glad to hear the good news," said Karen as she and Carlos slipped out into the street with Mike.

"Danny?"

"Yes. I can't wait to see the look on his face."

"Sure." Carlos grinned. "But what'll interest me, as an ugly devil boy, will be the look on *Joe's* face when we tell him about Dr. Purcell."

Karen quickened her pace.

"Thank goodness we have *something* to report." She glanced at the clock outside the bank. It read 12:47. "We should have been there nearly an hour ago. They'll be walking up the walls!"

6
Joe's First Night

Joe Armstrong and Danny Green were not exactly walking up the walls of the Williams house when the others got there. But they were pacing up and down the driveway with worried looks.

The worry turned to anger when Joe saw them.

"Where've you been?" he snapped. His was another voice that had the ring of command. He'd been head of his own construction company at the age of twenty-three. As a ghost, he wore with great pride the T-shirt with the stenciled words ARMSTRONG CONSTRUCTION across the chest. His hair was red, which perhaps partly explained his rather quick temper: Karen surmised, as she and Carlos walked toward him. "You should have been here at noon," he continued. "Wacko's been to the door about four times already."

"More," said Danny Green, glumly. He wore a black imitation-leather windbreaker and a red nylon scarf. But despite the jauntiness of his dress, he had a weary washed-out look for a kid of fourteen. "I kept count. It's been six times."

"That sounds like Wacko!" said Carlos. "Once every ten minutes. A very precise guy, Wacko Williams. I used to—"

"So?" Joe gave the word an angry drawn-out rasp. "What kept you?"

"We're sorry," said Karen. "But we've been visiting the sick."

"Don't be smart!" said Joe. "This is a serious—"

"It's true!" said Carlos. "We did like you said, Joe. We went among the shoppers downtown to see if any special scams were being worked—"

"And that's when we saw the invalid," said Karen.

Joe frowned.

"What invalid?"

"Hey!" said Danny. "You don't mean—?"

"Sure," said Karen. "Your Sylvia."

"Where?"

"Out in the street, Danny," said Carlos. "Wearing only a pair of yellow pajamas and nothing on her feet. That's what caught my eye."

"But it's OK," Karen said quickly, seeing the anguished way Danny was wringing his hands. "She's fine."

"Though it was touch and go at one point," said Carlos. "If I hadn't stalled the Malev who was stalking her."

"And if Dr. Purcell didn't finally put a stop to it," said Karen. "She's back in her body now, Danny. So relax."

Danny did relax then, just a little. Joe, however, seemed to have tightened up more.

"Did you say *Dr. Purcell*, Karen?" he asked.

"Yes."

"A little evil-looking guy in a tweed suit?"

"That's him!" said Carlos. "Do you know him, Joe?"

Without answering, Joe turned to Karen.

"You'd better tell us more! Everything. Right from the start."

He sounded so grave that Carlos forgot to keep glancing at the door. Judging from Joe's tone, it seemed like Carlos's original hunch had been right. It really did look as if the Ghost Squad might be on the brink of another major case. That being so, the two living members would have to continue to wait, until the ghosts had sorted out all the facts.

So Carlos joined Karen in making sure no detail was overlooked.

Danny and Joe listened in silence—apart from a deep sigh from Danny, when Karen described the way Sylvia's eyes had finally fluttered open.

"And that's about all," said Karen.

"Then we slipped out with Mike and came straight here."

"Thanks!" said Danny, grabbing first Karen's hand, then Carlos's. "Thanks, you guys!"

Joe nodded.

"Yes," he murmured. "You did well. Except—" He

shot Carlos a glance. Then shrugged. "But *you* couldn't have known."

"Except what?" said Carlos. "Couldn't have known what?"

"Except for mentioning Buzz," said Joe. "And *his* astral walking. You couldn't have known just how dangerous Purcell is."

"Do you—do you know him then?" said Carlos, glancing uneasily at Joe's deadly serious expression.

"I sure do!" Joe murmured. "He once propositioned *me*."

"Propositioned you?" said Karen.

"Yes. To join in his experiments. They're totally crazy, but—I don't know. From what you've just told me, it seems he's been making progress with them."

"When was this?" said Karen.

"Oh, a couple of years ago. When I first became a ghost. It—"

"Hey! Fellas! Are you there?"

The harsh whisper came from the doorway. A black kid with a thin serious face was peering out, but not seeing anything except the salted and sanded driveway, and the snow sparkling in the sun at the sides.

Carlos made up his mind. *He'd* be the one to have to transmit all this information to the others.

"Just ignore him," he said. "He'll be back in ten minutes. Let's get the full facts first. Go on, Joe."

The others nodded. Wacko groaned softly and closed the door. Joe continued.

It was a fascinating story. Not just because of Dr. Purcell's part in it, but also because this was the first

36

time they were getting to hear about Joe's experiences and feelings as a rookie ghost. Joe Armstrong, the knowledgeable and sympathetic leader who had done so much to help them when they'd been new to this strange afterlife!

"It was this time of the year, too," he said. "No snow, but cold, cold. I remember looking at my clothes, the ones I'd been wearing back in early September when—when it happened—and wondering why I didn't feel the cold."

They nodded. They all knew that first feeling. The feeling that something was very, very wrong. Sometimes it was the contrast between the weather conditions and their clothes, as in Joe's case. Sometimes it was the way everyone seemed to ignore them, as in Sylvia's. But the basic feeling was the same: a spookiness that quickly spilled over into panic.

"Where was this, Joe?" Danny asked. "When you came to?"

"Down by the railroad station, near where you lived." Joe grinned slightly. "Where you *really* lived at that time. I mean, *you* might have been one of the people who passed me by and didn't give me a glance."

Danny shivered.

"Yeah . . ."

"Anyway," said Joe, "one guy came along who gave me more than a glance. He was staring at the words on my shirt. Then he lifted his head, and those weird gray eyes of his looked right into mine, and he said, 'Why, you must be Joseph Armstrong himself!'"

"Did you know who *he* was?" Karen asked.

"Not at the time."

"Did you know *what* he was?" asked Carlos.

"Oh, sure! He told me himself in his very next words. 'Welcome to the club!' he said. 'You're a ghost too, now, old chap!' "

"Sounds warm and welcoming—for him," said Karen. "He didn't sound at all like that this morning."

"I don't doubt it," said Joe. "But he *can* make himself very charming. Part of his old bedside manner, I guess. . . . You see, he was a real medical doctor in his lifetime. Head of a very successful private nursing home. Specializing in old people. *Wealthy* old people."

Joe put such meaning into the word *wealthy* that Karen caught her breath.

"Hey—I remember something now! It was about five or six years ago. I was only a kid and didn't pay too much attention. But wasn't he the one who was accused of murdering some of his patients—giving them overdoses or something?"

"That was Purcell. Yes." Joe looked very grim. "The police were just closing in on him. One of the relatives who'd conspired with Purcell had confessed. In fact, Purcell was being pursued by a couple of patrol cars when he crashed. The guy he calls Muscle was with him. Muscle had been working at the home as a paramedic. Actually he was more of an accomplice and a bodyguard. They were both killed instantly, with about two million dollars in bonds and traveler's checks scattered all around them."

"Was Muscle there that night?" asked Carlos. "Your—uh—first night?"

Joe shook his head.

"No. I guess he only takes Muscle along when he's in an enforcing mood, not when he's scouting for guinea pigs."

"Guinea pigs?"

"Yeah," said Joe. "That's what he wanted me for. A guinea pig."

Carlos looked shocked.

"Like—like the Maggot guy?"

"Sure. Why not?" said Joe.

"But Maggot's a Malev! It's only Malevs who're interested in taking over living bodies! *You're* not a Malev, Joe!"

Joe smiled a queer crooked smile. It made Karen shudder. His next words made that shuddering increase.

"Oh, no? That's what *you* think!"

The other three glanced at each other—uneasy, two of them aghast.

Joe Armstrong? Their leader? A Malev?

7
Dr. Purcell's Proposition

Joe laughed.

"That's what you think and that's what you *know*, I hope! But Dr. Purcell had reason to think otherwise. After all, I *had* been murdered."

"And he thought—" Danny began.

"That I might be thirsting for revenge, yes," said Joe. "Anyway, he seemed to know a lot about my case. How it had been written off as an accident, though there were some who suggested it might be suicide.

" 'But my educated guess is that it was murder,' he told me, that night.

" 'Oh?' I said.

" 'But of course! The very fact that you are here now, as a ghost, proves it wasn't suicide. Suicides never come back as ghosts.' "

"Well, that was true anyway," said Karen. "But what made him so sure that it wasn't an accident?"

"I asked him that myself," said Joe. "And he said I was too experienced in the work, too fit, too *responsible* a kind of guy to meet with an accident like that on a perfectly calm day, and during a quiet period. Oh, he'd studied the evidence, all right! But I started wondering if he knew something else when he said, 'Wouldn't you like to find out who murdered you?'

" 'Wouldn't I ever!' I said. 'Who? Who was it?'

"He didn't answer me directly.

" 'Ah, but even if you did find out, what would you be able to do? *We* can't hurt living people. We can hardly make them feel us, no matter how hard we hit them. The most they feel is a faint cool brushing sensation, like the touch of a fly.' "

"Well, that's true enough," said Carlos.

"Of course it is," said Joe. "Don't forget, Dr. Purcell had already been a ghost for three years."

"What did you say, Joe?" Danny asked. "When he told you that."

"I said that I'd try to figure a way. But I was still waiting for an answer to my main question. 'Who was it?' I said. 'Do you know?' "

Joe sighed.

"But the little creep still kept me dangling. 'I'm *sure* you'd try to figure something out,' he said. 'You look like a very determined young man. But you still wouldn't get far. Not without—'

"Then he broke off and stared into the distance.

" 'Without what?' I said. 'And for Pete's sake, who *was* my murderer?'

"He looked me straight in the eyes again.

" 'I don't know,' he said. 'I wish I did. But just imagine. If you had expert help in taking possession of a living body—why, *then* you'd be able to do justice to your murderer. Maim him! Kill him!' "

Joe winced.

"I don't think I've ever seen a more evil, gloating look on anybody's face. Much as I wanted, and still want, to identify my killer and get justice done, I wasn't full of *that* kind of hatred. This guy's a nut! I thought.

" 'Anyway,' I said, 'I'd still have to find out who it was, and maybe as a ghost I'll have a better chance.'

" 'Oh, yes!' he said. 'But you can't have it both ways, Joseph. But suppose I was to tell you that someone is working on the problems of possession, and has almost perfected a means of enabling you to maintain contact with other ghosts while still in possession of a living body—'

" 'Who?' I said. 'What someone?'

"The puckers and wrinkles began to squirm.

" 'You're looking at him!' he said."

"So what did you say then?" murmured Carlos.

"Well," said Joe, "then I *knew* he was nuts. Also dangerous. So I told him I'd think about it. And that seemed to satisfy him. 'As soon as you're ready, Joseph,' he said.

"Then I went on my way and stayed clear of him ever since. Luckily, he's so busy—with his investigations and experiments, I guess—you don't often see him around."

"Where does he hang out, then?" said Danny.

"Hawkins Station is one of his—uh—haunts," said Joe.

The others nodded. It seemed a likely place. It had once been the first stop on an old branch railroad line, long since abandoned. The tracks had been pulled up, and the weeds allowed to thrive. The building itself had first been used as a storage shed by a local farmer. Then it had been bought by an amateur theatrical group. Plays had been staged there for a couple of years, in summer. Then that too had folded, and for the past five years it had stood empty— except for an occasional bunch of partying teenagers, innumerable mice and rats and bats and, apparently, a few furtive and exceedingly malicious ghosts.

"You said that was just one of his hangouts," said Carlos. "Where else?"

"Somewhere quite the opposite," said Joe. "He must use the station as some kind of—uh—workshop. I've heard he spends a lot of time in places like the Lakeview Hotel, mingling with the living guests, listening to their conversations, watching TV."

"Have you seen much of him, since?" Karen asked.

"Just glimpses. Sometimes with Muscle. Sometimes—especially in the last twelve months—another guy."

"The one they call Maggot?" asked Carlos.

"No. Not according to your description, anyway. This is a little guy. Very quiet. Gray-haired and dressed in gray." Joe looked thoughtful. "Maybe he's another doctor or a scientist of some kind."

"Why?" said Carlos, looking up sharply. "What makes you think that?"

Joe shrugged.

"Oh, I don't know. . . . Just—well—" His look hardened into one of deep concern. "Like I said, from what you've just told me—Purcell sounds as if he's really made some big advances in his experiments."

"He certainly sounded very sure of himself," said Karen.

"And very scientific," said Carlos.

"And that's what worries me," said Joe. "It sounds like he might be ready for a big breakthrough."

"Like—like *our* breakthrough?" Karen gulped, remembering that mesh of wrinkles, those cold eyes, that turtlelike snapping mouth. "Except for *bad* purposes?"

Joe nodded.

"Exactly. So we'd better alert the others. Buzz especially."

"Here's Wacko again," said Danny.

This time the ghosts didn't hang back. All four were at Wacko's side before he'd had the chance to repeat his whispered question for the eighth time.

8
Wacko's Bogeyman

"Hey, are you—?" Wacko began.

It was Carlos who touched him on the right ear. Wacko breathed a deep sigh and muttered, "Thank goodness!"

Just as Dr. Purcell had described, the tap had come through as nothing more than a barely perceptible brushing. But Wacko had been expecting it, and that made all the difference.

"Are you all inside?" he whispered.

This time Carlos touched him on the left ear. Joe was still taking a last look around outside.

"All clear," said Joe, stepping in.

"*Now* are you all inside?" Wacko whispered.

Joe himself gave him the touch on the right ear, meaning yes.

Wacko closed the door.

"You said you'd be here at—"

Wacko's whisper was interrupted by his mother's voice.

"Henry, is that *you?*"

"Yes, Mom."

"*Again?*"

Mrs. Williams appeared at the kitchen door.

"Yes, Mom."

"Why do you keep going to the door? It must be at least ten times in the past hour!"

"Eight, Mom."

"So what's with you? Are you expecting someone? I thought Buzz had arrived hours ago."

"Yes, Mom. It's the snow."

"Snow?"

"It's an assignment. Science. To study snow in all its forms."

"You and your science! Snow is snow. There's only one form—white and cold."

"Not so, Mom. . . ."

"Oh, boy!" muttered Carlos, dancing on the bottom stairs with impatience. "Now we'll be here all day!"

It certainly began to seem like it.

"The Indians in these parts used to say there were forty different kinds—depending on temperature, wind direction and all sorts of other factors. The Eskimos have identified eighty different kinds."

"If he says one word more, I'll give him the red alert sign!" growled Carlos.

He raised his hand, ready to tap Wacko's top lip,

but it was unnecessary. Mrs. Williams cut the lecture short with a hollow-sounding, "Eighty? I'll be darned!" and went quickly back into the kitchen before her son could go into details.

Wacko's room was on the third floor. It was long and low-ceilinged, with a bed and a chest of drawers and other bedroom furniture at one end, and a table under the window at the other. In front of the table were a couple of upright chairs. Buzz Phillips got up as soon as Wacko entered.

"Any luck?"

"Yeah. At last!"

"All of them?"

"As far as I know."

Buzz's face brightened. He was a year younger than Wacko, but taller and huskier. His broad mouth assumed its normally good-humored smile, and his deep-set brown eyes glowed as he stared at the seemingly empty space beyond Wacko.

"Hi, you guys! Been Christmas shopping?"

None of them bothered to touch him. Now that they were in their headquarters, the ghosts had a much better means of communicating.

They'd all turned to the table. In the center was a rather roughly finished word processor, its screen glowing a soft green. It was roughly finished because it had been assembled by Wacko and Carlos, when Carlos was alive. And while they hadn't spent much time making it look good on the outside, the design of the circuitry was one of the most sophisticated yet known.

Carlos was standing in front of the word processor now. Even as a kid of thirteen, he'd been regarded by his teachers and other grownups as a scientific genius. Wacko himself was no slouch in that department, but he was always the first to admit that compared to Carlos he was still a baby.

Carlos turned to Joe.

"Shall I start?"

"Sure. Go ahead."

There was a hush in Joe's voice. It was always the same on these occasions. The other ghosts felt the tension, too, and so did the two living boys.

Would Carlos be able to work the miracle yet again?

Carlos turned back to the word processor. His own tension was different—springier, less static. To him, it wasn't a miracle. To him, it was simply directing the micro-micro-energy that all ghosts have into the right channels.

And he, Carlos Gomez, knew precisely where those channels were, and every intricacy of their structure, their relationships, their energy needs. Hadn't he designed them?

His chest swelled. The letters and symbols at the edge of the daisy-wheel logo began to quiver as the T-shirt was stretched. He raised his hands, then let the fingers droop, a few inches above the keyboard. He was like a concert pianist preparing to strike the first notes. His body went very still, rigid. Danny closed his eyes. He could never get used to the strain of watching this preliminary gathering of forces—feeling every time that this might be the moment when those forces would desert his friend.

Then Danny heard a long-drawn sigh. He opened his eyes.

And yes, the screen was flickering. As Carlos's fingers danced above the keys, never touching them, never physically moving them at all, the letters and words began to form.

> *"The full Ghost Squad is now present. Stand by for some very important news."*

Karen was the one who'd sighed with relief. And as she watched, she wondered if Dr. Purcell's breakthrough—whatever it was—could ever be compared to *this*.

She hoped not.

Since making their breakthrough, six months ago, the Ghost Squad members had used their powers and capabilities for nothing but good purposes. They had saved an elderly couple from being robbed and killed; they had thwarted the attempts of a murderous con man to cheat Danny's mother out of her compensation money; they had uncovered a terrorist bomb plot; they had prevented a nasty attempt to spike Halloween candy;

and they had even helped to track down a vicious war criminal. And these were just the highlights.

Karen couldn't imagine the reptilian doctor doing any of those things.

He'd have been on the side of the robbers, the thugs, the murderers. *His* bunch would have been the exact evil opposite of the Ghost Squad.

"Of *course* it's important news!" she said when Wacko turned and said, "It had better be very important, keeping us waiting all this time!"

Wacko couldn't hear her, but he certainly read Carlos's reply on the screen:

"Dummy! It's the most important news you'll have heard all year!"

"Just the facts, Carlos," Joe said quietly.

Carlos nodded and turned back to the keyboard.

"The Ghost Squad could soon face the biggest threat ever! So how d'you like them crackers, huh? How—"

"Carlos!" said Joe.

"Sorry!" muttered Carlos.

But he had the others' attention now. Both Buzz and Wacko were staring, openmouthed.

"Starting with the bare facts then," Carlos transmitted. *"We—Karen and I—while patrolling downtown looking for Christmas scams, as promised, met, at around 11:57 (for those who like their facts precise), a guy, a ghost, name of Purcell, Dr. Purcell. He—"*

There was a crash. It was Wacko's chair. He'd turned around so fast.

"Him?"

Buzz stared at Wacko. So did the ghosts.

"Do you know him, then?" Buzz asked.

"*Of* him, yes! I know *of* him!" Wacko grinned sheepishly. "I'm sorry!" he murmured. "But—wow! It took me by surprise."

"Why?" said Buzz. "I mean why the shock?"

"It's just—well—Dr. Purcell was a kind of bogeyman in this house. About five years ago."

"A bogeyman?"

"Yeah. You see, Dad had just started working in the state's attorney's office and this was his first big case. Dr. Purcell had been suspected of murder. And Dad had been in charge of gathering the evidence." Wacko looked up. "Hey, I'm sorry! I shouldn't be interrupting your report and—"

"*GO ON!!!*"

Carlos, through the screen, had said it for them all.

"Well—" Wacko shrugged. "Nothing came of it. Just when he was about to be arrested, the guy was killed in a car crash. And—and—well—you're going to think this is crazy—but he hated Dad, really hated him. He'd tried to bribe Dad to drop the charges, and Dad wouldn't hear of it—just added the bribery charge to the others."

"So what's crazy about that?" said Buzz.

"Nothing. It was me. I was only ten and I said, 'Hey, Dad, now that he's dead, maybe he'll come back and haunt you!' "

Everyone was staring at Wacko.

"So—so what did your dad say?" whispered Buzz.

"He just made a joke of it. Used to say things like, 'Hey, Henry! You don't eat your broccoli and Doc Purcell will come and get you!' "

Wacko smiled.

Karen shivered, seeing that turtle face again.

Then Wacko's smile faded, and he too gave a little shudder.

"Of course, I didn't really believe in ghosts. *Then*."

"No," said Buzz, thoughtfully. He turned to where he thought the ghosts were standing. "You'd better tell us more about this guy!"

"Yeah," said Wacko. "Tell us exactly what happened. How you came to meet *him!*"

"Go ahead, Carlos," Joe said. Then, looking very grave, he murmured, "This puts a whole new complexion on the case!"

9
Plans of Action

For the next fifteen minutes, Carlos's fingers were busy. The green light flickered on the faces of Buzz and Wacko. Once or twice, Buzz opened his mouth, then slowly closed it without uttering a word.

Even the ghosts hadn't anything to say. Carlos had decided to tell the morning's story exactly as it happened, and he left nothing out. So he described the crowd outside Dino's, the kid in the pajamas, the arrival of Santa, the intrusion of Maggot, and Dr. Purcell's intervention. Finally Carlos passed on everything Joe had told them about *his* meeting with Dr. Purcell and the glimpses he'd had of the man later.

When Carlos had reached that point, he turned.

"I guess that covers everything?"

"Nice work, Carlos," Joe murmured.

"It seems to have stunned those two," said Karen.

"Is there any wonder?" said Joe. "What with Buzz being a potential donor and Wacko a likely target for attack, it could get very nasty."

Danny was just about to say something when Buzz said, "Who *was* this Maggot creep supposed to be stalking, anyway?"

Carlos turned to Karen. She shook her head.

"He didn't say."

"Maybe not directly," said Joe. "But my guess is Tommy Peck."

"Who's Tommy Peck?" said Danny.

"The guy playing Santa," said Joe. "It sounds like him, from Carlos's description. And Tommy is one of Dino's lame ducks—a reformed thief and a longtime alcoholic."

After Carlos had transmitted this new information, Wacko nodded.

"That would figure," he said. "Someone whose astral body is likely to take a walk when he's dead drunk."

"Which means that *he's* at the top of Purcell's hit list right now," said Buzz. "Before he turns his attention to—uh—other kinds of astral walkers."

"Anyway," said Wacko, "what can *we* be doing, Buzz and I? This sounds like a ghost-versus-ghost matter."

"Tell him," said Joe, with a glint in his eye, "this . . ."

And a few seconds later, Carlos was transmitting Joe's instructions.

"*You can be finding out more about Tommy Peck's move-*

ments. Have a word with Dino himself. He owes us, after our help in the Halloween affair."

The two living boys looked so eager that Joe quickly had Carlos adding a caution.

"*But be careful! If any of Purcell's bunch overhear you making inquiries about their next donor, they'll get suspicious. And Maggot's likely to be somewhere around.*"

"Muscle, too," Karen added. "It struck me that Purcell isn't likely to allow Maggot to goof off again. They'll be keeping tabs on him."

"She's right," murmured Carlos. "Want me to tell Buzz and Wacko that?"

Joe shook his head.

"No point in making them *too* nervous. We'll be covering them, but—"

Wacko interrupted.

"Sure," he said, looking worried. "We'll be discreet. But how will we know when this Maggot's around?"

Carlos transmitted Joe's answer.

"*Two of us will be there. We'll give you the red alert signal, if necessary.*"

"Which two?" said Buzz.

Joe was thinking hard.

"No. Make that *three*, Carlos. You, Karen and Danny. One to be ready to give the alert, one to watch Maggot and distract his attention, if necessary—and one to watch out for Muscle or any other Malev."

"Good thinking," said Karen while Carlos was transmitting this amendment. "Something tells me we can't be too careful."

"Yeah!" grunted Danny. "And how about you, Joe? Won't you be coming along?"

Joe was smiling.

"No, Danny."

"But if there's trouble! If the Muscle guy—"

"I know, I know. But you'll just have to take care of it yourselves. No—don't look disappointed. I'm not chickening out. It's just that I've decided it's time we found out more about Purcell's plans. The progress he's made. His methods. How many—uh—Prowling Hermits he has around him."

"Hey! I like that!" said Carlos, turning from the word processor. "Prowling Hermits! Yeah!"

"Anyway," said Danny, "how do we find all *that* out?"

Joe smiled the crooked Malev smile again.

"We find out," he said, in a low matching voice, "because I will ask."

Carlos's eyes widened.

"But—"

"I've just decided," said Joe, in the same tone and with the leer broadening, "that it's time at last to take Dr. Purcell up on his proposition." He looked around at the other three ghosts and laughed. "To go under-cover, dummies! As a potential Prowling Hermit, my-self!"

10
Santa's Helpers

It was busy inside Dino's that afternoon. Dino was presiding on the low platform at the side of the checkout, on a spindly stool, keeping watch on everything and everybody from under the visor of his cap.

"Maybe he's too busy to talk with us," said Wacko, frowning, when they entered the store.

"It sure looks that way," Buzz murmured.

Dino didn't go in for fancy furnishings. There weren't even any real counters—just upturned crates and packing cases, with the merchandise displayed on top: toasters, blenders, carpet slippers, running shoes, transistor radios, miniature TV sets, board games, computer games, electric irons, neckties, makeup kits, shavers, cuddly toy animals, baseball bats, catchers' mitts, footballs, frying pans, microwave ovens, underwear, outerwear, dog collars, cute little cloth mice stuffed with catnip—something for everyone in every family.

Normally, there wasn't much room, but today— what with the extra goods on display and the Christmas bargain hunters—the store seemed crowded to bursting point. And, making it even more congested, almost one quarter of the floor space was taken up by what looked like a decorator's scaffolding, complete with screens and draped sheets.

But no painters were at work behind those white and pale greenish blue walls. As Wacko and Buzz got closer, they realized what this edifice—a cross between a cavern hewn out of a glacier and an ice palace—was supposed to be. There was a sign to prove it: FAIRY GROTTO ☞ THIS WAY TO SEE SANTA. And there was also a guard: a surly, self-conscious checkout girl dressed in a Santa Claus hat, a red lumber jacket and red tights.

She glowered at Buzz as, grinning, he nudged Wacko.

"Do *you* want to see Santa, sonny?" she snapped.

Buzz blushed.

"Take it easy, Sue!" he said. "I was only admiring your costume."

"Get lost!" she growled. Then she grinned, too, or rather smiled radiantly as she saw Dino's eyes turned in her direction. "Sorry, boys, but only under-tens allowed in here. Unless you're accompanying one."

"Come on!" murmured Wacko. "We're here to talk with Dino."

At first, Dino looked as if he was going to treat them as brusquely as the girl.

"What are you looking for?" he grunted, his eyes still flitting around.

"Nothing, Dino," said Buzz. "We just wanted—"

"So beat it! I'm busy!"

"Hey, Dino!" said Wacko. "This is *us*, remember? The guys—"

"The guys who helped clear up that Halloween mess. Sure I remember. But this is no time for a social call. OK?"

"Well, it isn't exactly a social call, Dino."

For a couple of seconds, the eyes rested on Buzz. "So?"

"So we just wanted to ask about Tommy Peck."

The eyes blazed briefly.

"*That* bum!" Dino growled. "*What* about him? You doing some amateur detective work again?"

"No—uh—not exactly. I mean—"

"Because problem he may be, but he's *my* problem, not the town's." Dino's eyes softened a little. "What I'm saying is this. If you think Tommy's up to his old thieving tricks again, forget it."

"We weren't thinking that. We—"

"I wish I could say the same about his drinking," Dino went on, gazing at the grotto. "It's a lot easier to get a guy to go straight than a drunk to go dry and stay dry. Especially under stress . . . like *now!*"

A bellow from the grotto had caused Dino to break his sentence. The bellow of, "*Cut that out, kid!*"

"Sue!" Dino yelled. "Get in there! Quick!"

Dino turned to the boys.

"Look! I don't have time to—" Then his look of

annoyance faded. A slow smile began to spread. "Hey! I'll tell you what. If you guys have nothing else to do— Excuse me! Wait there!"

Dino got off the stool with startling agility. How he managed to cross that crowded store so rapidly baffled the boys. One second he'd been sitting on the stool, and the next second he was at the entrance to the grotto, picking up a tearful five-year-old boy and transforming those tears to smiles with a few quick words and a candy bar. Then he came back to his stool.

"Yeah," he said. "I was telling you about the idea I just had."

"Involving us?" said Wacko.

"Involving you—right! You see, it's no use blaming Sue. She can't be in two places at once—guarding the entrance and in there with Tommy. And it's no use blaming him—much. Dealing with kids is no easy job, especially when they're all excited. So . . ." Dino grinned as he looked from Wacko to Buzz and back to Wacko. "So why don't *you* be in there? Just to keep order."

"Us?" said Wacko.

"As *bouncers?*" said Buzz.

Dino's eyes flashed again.

"Bouncers nothing! When I say to keep order, I mean for you to handle things smoothly. And you could also take notes."

"Notes?"

"Yeah. Like what the kids want for Christmas. Kinda survey. You know. Market research."

60

Buzz looked at Wacko. Wacko was staring at Dino.
"But—"

"As Santa's *helpers*," said Dino, beaming. "Like part of the act. Here—" He reached into an open cardboard box. Buzz had noticed it earlier and guessed that it contained Christmas decorations—some rich red, others frosty white. Well, he'd been right. In a way. He gaped as Dino drew out a pair of Santa Claus hats. "Try these for size."

"Us?"

"Wear *them?*"

"Sure!" Dino was dipping into the box again. "There's some coats in here. Miles too big for Sue or any of the other girls, but—*there!*"

"Sorry!" said Wacko.

"Huh-uh!" grunted Buzz.

"Hey, come on, fellas!" said Dino. "Not for two-fifty an hour?"

"I wouldn't do it," said Wacko, "for ten dol—"

"OK! OK!" said Dino. "*Four* dollars an hour?"

"I still—"

It was then that Wacko felt the touches.

Buzz was putting a hand to *his* right ear already.

The boys looked at each other.

Of course!

From the Ghost Squad's point of view, the job would be perfect!

Wacko sighed. Buzz shrugged.

Each of them felt another flurry of touches on the right ear.

"OK," said Wacko.

"Sure," grunted Buzz.

"Terrific!" said Dino, looking happier than he had all day.

Sue's smile was genuine enough as Dino and the two new helpers entered the grotto.

"So you *did* want to see Santa?" she said.

Buzz felt glad that no kids over ten were allowed in there. He'd have hated for some of the guys from school to see him in that hat and coat.

Wacko was looking just as miserable.

Once inside the entrance, however, their embarrassment faded. To get to the inner chamber, they had first to thread their way along a labyrinthine passageway formed out of screens—a route that kept doubling back on itself.

"This makes it look bigger," Dino explained. "A real clever use of space."

He was taking his time, stopping to admire the embellishments and see what sort of impression was being made on the new recruits.

"Nice job, huh?"

"Uh—yeah! Sure . . . sure!" said Wacko, with a look of awe.

"You bet!" mumbled Buzz.

At first, it seemed that Santa needed no extra helpers. The passageway was thronged with fairies—strange fairies, as tall as human adults—two or three at every turn. But on closer inspection they turned out to be store-window dummies, dressed in ballet skirts and equipped with makeshift wands.

"I got 'em cheap," said Dino. "Big New York fashion store that was burned down."

Buzz nodded. That explained why they looked so weird.

Because, despite the wands and the frills, these skinny, haughty, strutting fairies looked more likely to cast evil spells than grant wishes.

Dino must have mistaken the boys' silence for awed admiration.

"Wait until you see the elves!" he said, pausing at the last corner, where a fairy—skinnier, haughtier and more glittering than the rest—was lit up from crown to toes by a spotlight.

Dino waved the bedazzled Buzz and Wacko through into the central chamber.

Tommy Peck, sitting on a thronelike armchair, peered gloomily out at them from behind a very bushy white beard.

"Hi, Dino!" he muttered. "Sorry I lost my temper a while back. The kid seemed to think all these were for him."

With a sweep of a gnarled nicotine-stained hand, he indicated dozens of gift-wrapped packages strewn at his feet.

"That's OK, Tommy," said Dino. "See—I brought you some help."

Santa glanced at the boys and sniffed.

"What's wrong, Dino! Don't you trust me not to—?"

"Sure, sure, Tommy! Sure, I trust you. It's just that *anyone* would need help, where there's kids coming and going all day."

"Yeah, well—it's kinda slack right now."

"Maybe," said Dino, "but it won't stay this way. . . . Well, fellas, how d'you like the elves? I got these cheap, too. Bankrupt garden center."

Buzz and Wacko had been gaping at the elves that were swarming all over that inner room—in every corner, behind the throne, on shelves. Had they been doing Santa-type things—hammering, sawing, dipping into pots of glue or paint and generally helping to get the toys ready—they might not have looked so odd. But Dino's explanation had been quite unnecessary. These were obviously garden gnomes. They always had been and always would be just a bunch of loafers: fishing in thin air; gossiping, cross-legged, on the tops of plastic mushrooms; or simply snoozing, with their hands folded over bulging paunches. One was even sitting back on *his* mushroom, swigging greedily from a bottle.

Tommy's faded blue eyes kept straying to this one as Dino introduced the boys.

"Coupla good kids—they'll take care of any trouble."

"Sure, sure . . ."

"You'll be able to concentrate better, Tommy."

"Sure, Dino. Look—quit fussin'. You make me nervous when you keep fussin'."

"I'm sorry, Tommy, but—well—"

"I know what you're thinking, Dino, and I keep telling you, I'll be OK."

"Sure?" said Dino, glancing at the drinking gnome, then back at Tommy.

"Sure I'm sure! Hey, and while I think of it, will it be OK if I borrow this outfit, next weekend?"

Dino shrugged.

"No problem. But—what for? You'll be working *here* with it."

"I mean after hours." The faded eyes lit up briefly. "I got me a special engagement—evenings. Carmen's Cookery. They're hiring me for the big after-dinner sleigh ride they're running. Sleigh Ride with Santa."

Dino grunted.

"Always some new gimmick. . . . But, sure you can borrow the outfit, Tommy. So long as—uh—"

"Oh, I'll take care of it! Don't worry about that, Dino."

"I wasn't," said Dino. "Anyway, I'll leave you guys to get acquainted."

When he'd gone, Tommy winked.

"Great guy, Dino—but just like a mother hen." He laughed. "And me old enough to be his father, too!" Chuckling, he began to fumble under his robe. "Notice how he didn't care for me taking the Carmen's Cookery job? He thinks I might be tempted—all them hot rum toddies flowing."

At last he drew out a flat metal flask. Rather shakily, he began to unscrew the cap.

"He thinks I might start drinking again! Heh, heh!"

"Well, aren't you already?" said Wacko as Tommy put the flask to his lips.

"Nargh!" said Tommy. "This is cough medicine. Here—sniff!"

Wacko backed away.

"Huh—yeah. It *smells* like cough medicine, anyway."

"And so it is," said Tommy, replacing the cap and thrusting the flask out of sight. "I need it for my throat. Talking to all these kids."

At that moment, the next customer came in—a little girl accompanied by her mother. As Tommy bent to receive her hushed greetings and requests, Wacko turned to Buzz.

"What d'you think?" he whispered.

"*Was* it cough medicine?"

"I think so. But I remember reading someplace that for ex-alcoholics it's often the first step back."

"Dino didn't seem thrilled about the Carmen's Cookery job."

"I'm not surprised. There's always a lot of drinking going on there. And on Christmas weekend—well!"

"I bet that'll be good news to—" Buzz broke off, feeling Wacko's sharp nudge. "Uh—to you-know-who," he whispered. "Hey, and relax, Wacko! If one of *them* was around, we'd be getting the red alert. Right, guys?"

A faint brush on the right ear confirmed his hunch. Wacko received one also, and he did relax.

But not fully.

It wouldn't be long before they had a visit from Maggot, he felt sure. And, when they did, would Carlos and the others be able to handle the situation without giving too much away? In *that* confined space?

Wacko wasn't the only one to be bothered by this. Already, twenty minutes earlier, as the boys were being ushered into Santa's presence, Karen had spotted the snag.

"Well, that settles it," she said, after glancing around and noticing there was no place for anyone as big as Maggot to be hiding. "Danny, *you'll* have to be the one who stays in here."

"Why me?" said Danny. "I haven't even seen this Maggot guy. How will I know it's him? I mean, I don't want to blow it!"

"You can't mistake him," said Karen.

Once again, she described the Hermit.

"And watch out for the one white tooth," said Carlos. "It *looks* like a maggot. Crawling out of a hunk of cheese!"

Danny frowned.

"Sure, but since you've both seen him, why doesn't one of *you* stay and give the alert?"

"Talk sense, Danny!" said Carlos. "As soon as he sees either me or Karen, he'll get suspicious. After the trouble we gave him this morning."

"And we wouldn't be able to hide from him in *here*," said Karen.

Danny nodded.

"Yeah . . . I guess you're right."

"We won't be far away, though," said Karen. "When he arrives, one of us will be following him. We can always finger him from the corner, behind his back."

She nodded toward the inner chamber's entrance, where the last of the fairies was already doing some pointing.

"*Which* one of you?" asked Danny.

"I will," said Karen.

"You?" said Carlos.

"Yes. Because I'm the one less likely to attract his attention. You were the one who actually fought with him, remember?"

Carlos nodded.

"Yeah. It makes sense. But where does that leave *me*?"

"Out in the store," said Karen, firmly. "Mingling with the crowd. Keeping watch for any spy Dr. Purcell might send to keep tabs on him . . . OK? Satisfied now, Danny?"

Danny was looking relieved.

"I just didn't want to blow it," he said. "That's all."

Danny's assignment turned out to be more interesting than he'd expected. For one thing, it gave him the opportunity to study the Prowling Hermits' potential victim. For another thing, it was always pleasant to work with the two living members of the squad—one of whom had been his best friend in life. And then there was the procession of kids—a procession that picked up in numbers throughout the next hour or so.

There were even a few ghosts who drifted in, too. Danny gave each of these a close look. He knew it wasn't always easy to spot a Malev. Usually it was, of course. Once these vicious, vengeful beings became ghosts, they tended to drop the protective disguises that made them so extra-dangerous in life: the phony meekness or friendliness they'd hidden their true nature behind. Most of them didn't bother to keep this up as ghosts, knowing that they were invisible now to the living people they still hated and wished—oh, so fiercely—to hurt.

But, Danny thought, you never know. Especially when Malevs are operating against other ghosts.

At first, the ghosts that entered Santa's inner sanctum seemed a pretty regular bunch. Some had obviously come in out of curiosity; others out of concern. The concerned ones were relatives of the living kids who were visiting Santa Claus: mainly grandparents. Danny could recognize these by the way they hovered protectively, wincing if the kids showed signs of misbehaving, smiling if they said something cute. There were even a few older brothers or sisters—ghosts who, like Danny himself, had been responsible during their lives for the protection and well-being of the younger kids.

The high spot came late in the afternoon, when Danny's own brothers and sister turned up.

Danny's heart gave a lurch when he saw them: Mike and Jilly, with Arnie between them, holding hands—Jilly dragging slightly as she turned to stare at the last fairy; Mike looking self-conscious; Arnie wide-eyed and hushed.

They all had their new shiny quilted jackets on—three purple pumpkins with clean frost-flushed faces sticking out. Danny was pleased to see the older pair looking so bright. Only Arnie had the drawn, anxious, bewildered look that Danny knew of old. Arnie had always been the one most like Danny himself.

"Well, well!" said Santa, bending forward. "I bet *you* three aren't brothers and sister!"

Jilly shot him a scornful look.

"We are too! We—"

She was pulled up by a nudge from Mike.

"Sorry!" she said, lowering her eyes. "Sorry—uh—Mister Claus."

"That's OK, honey," said Santa. "And you can drop the *Mister* . . ." He sat back, hands on knees, relaxed but attentive—all that a Santa should be. "So tell me—what would you like me to bring you for Christmas?"

They all started talking at once.

"Hey! Hey!" said Santa. "Ladies first!"

Jilly frowned.

"I ain't a lady! I'm a *girl!*"

"Girls, then," said Santa, winking at Buzz and Wacko, who were standing by, notebooks and pens poised.

Jilly turned to look at them. Then started.

"Hey, I know *him!* And—"

She broke off, when Arnie piped up, gazing solemnly at Santa.

"Sylvia's a girl, but she couldn't come. She's sick."

"Oh dear!" said Santa, speaking gently. "Is it serious?"

Danny could have hugged Tommy just then, for the real concern that showed in those faded blue eyes.

This guy gets taken over by a Hermit over my—uh—dead body! he vowed.

Jilly answered the question.

"Yeah. But she'll be OK now."

"Is she in the hospital?"

"No, at home," said Mike. "Mom's taking care of her."

"But she *almost* died!" Jilly insisted. "Mom said she was in a comic!"

"A *coma!*" Mike said.

"A comma, then!" snapped Jilly.

"My goodness!" said Santa. He turned to his helpers. "We must make sure *she* gets something special!"

"Our brother Danny really did die!" Arnie piped up again.

Mike's and Jilly's shoulders slumped. They nodded sadly.

"Gee!" Tommy murmured. "That's too bad!" Then his voice brightened. "But who knows? He might be watching over you all, right now, this very minute, listening to everything you say."

The kids looked up at the ceiling—doubt in Mike's and Jilly's eyes, vague hope in Arnie's. Danny didn't know whether he wanted to laugh or cry. Buzz and Wacko looked at each other and grinned awkwardly.

Then Jilly pointed to Buzz.

"*He* was Danny's best friend. Weren't you?"

Buzz nodded.

"Anyway," said Santa, "let's have those lists now. You first, young lady. . . ."

And it was then, while Jilly was placing her order, that Danny suddenly became aware of another presence.

He turned—and felt a kind of electric shock tingle through his limbs.

Tall guy—yes.

Long leather coat—yes.

Tall fur hat—yes.

Flabby face, mustache, heavy-lidded eyes—yes, yes, yes.

And those heavy-lidded eyes were staring intently at Jilly.

Danny blinked. Somewhere behind the newcomer there'd been a quick movement. The fairy at the corner seemed to have acquired a second right arm, a finger of which was stab-stab-stabbing toward the leather-clad back. Then Karen's head appeared.

"It's—him!" she mouthed.

Very, very slightly, Danny nodded. He looked back at the man—and received another shock. This time those hooded eyes were staring at *him!*

"Who d'ya think *you're* staring at?" snarled the light husky voice. The eyes lurched back in Jilly's direction, as if the stranger were hypnotized by the little girl. It suddenly occurred to Danny that it must have been Jilly's resemblance to Sylvia. What must have fascinated the guy was this larger version of the kid whose body he'd been cheated out of, earlier. "Well?"

The eyes were back on Danny.

Danny suddenly felt angry.

"I've as much right to be here as *you!*"

"Oh, yeah?"

The stranger took a step forward, his hands rising and opening and aimed toward Danny's neck.

"I—I'm sorry!" said Danny.

He'd remembered his real mission.

The man paused.

"So beat it!"

At the word *beat*, the teeth were bared. And—yes—there was the one white tooth in among all the yellow.

"Hey! It's that Maggot creep!"

Danny was just as startled as Maggot at the voice from the entrance.

Carlos's head had replaced Karen's, peering around the corner—peering and jeering.

Danny darted toward Buzz, hoping to give the red alert while the Malev's back was turned. But before he'd reached the other side of Santa's chair, he was arrested by another voice.

Maggot had been saying to Carlos, "*You* again!" as he stepped toward the entrance. "I been hoping I might see *you!*"

Then had come the new voice:

"Cut it out, Maggot! Get on with your job! I'll t-take care of th-these two l-later!"

Danny stared. White jacket, black open-necked shirt, gold cross, dark glasses. And those shoulders!

This had to be the one called Muscle.

He was pointing toward Santa and the little group around him.

"*That's* who you're supposed t-to be watching, you j-jerk!"

Maggot humbly turned. Now the eyes of both Hermits were turned in Tommy's direction. And Tommy's direction included Buzz's and Wacko's.

How to give the red alert *now?*

Danny thought quickly.

When he was alive, he'd been considered by his teachers and most of his classmates to be pretty dumb. But *then* he'd had so many things to distract his thoughts: his anxiety over his brothers and sisters, feelings of hunger or indigestion, great tiredness often, a whole raft of itches and chafings and pinchings from ill-fitting clothes and shoes. But as a ghost he'd suffered from none of these, and he often surprised himself by the sharpness of his unimpeded intelligence.

He surprised himself now. He baffled the two Malevs. And he actually shocked Karen and Carlos, who'd crept back to take a peek at what was happening.

"You jerk!" he screamed. "You dirty, rotten, lousy jerk! *You* caused my death! *You* got me to explore that stinking ruin of a factory! *You're* no friend of mine!"

And what really shocked Karen and Carlos was his target.

"I could kill ya!" Danny screamed, lashing out at Buzz.

Then: "Well, I'll be darned!" Carlos murmured, suddenly grinning.

Danny's lashing out hadn't been as wild as it looked. The swinging fist was aimed at Buzz's top lip.

Wham! Wham! Wham!

Buzz stopped writing and slowly lifted his pen to his lip, scratching it as if he'd felt a fly brush against it. Then, with a glance at Wacko, he went on writing.

The red alert had been delivered.

"Hey, kid!" Muscle jeered. "Cool it! You'll never hurt a living person that way!"

"No!" growled Maggot, catching sight of Carlos and

Karen. "But you *can* hurt another ghost, and those two have been spying on me. They're ruining my concentration. And *you're* supposed to be covering me!"

The sneer vanished from Muscle's face. He looked at Maggot as if he could have torn his head off. Then he must have realized that what Maggot was saying was true.

"S-sure!" he snarled, with murder still in his eyes as he turned and ran, fast on the heels of Karen and Carlos.

11
Hawkins Station

Around the time that Buzz and Wacko were being hired as Santa's helpers, Joe was on his way to Hawkins Station. He'd already taken a quick look around the Lakeview Hotel and, seeing no signs of Dr. Purcell there, he'd decided that the disused station would be the next most likely place.

Hawkins Station was about three miles from town by the shortest route—following the line of the old railroad—but this didn't bother Joe. He knew that whenever he did meet up with Purcell, he'd better have his undercover story just right. The slightest hint that Joe was not telling the truth would set the alarm bells ringing behind those cold eyes. The walk to Hawkins Station—through the town's outskirts and into the quiet rolling fields—would give him the opportunity to go over his story again and again.

It was certainly a pleasant day for a walk. Had it been blowing a hurricane, it wouldn't have affected a ghost much physically. But mentally it might have distracted him. Joe knew how easy it was for ghosts to forget they were ghosts and be completely thrown by conditions they knew would surely have thrown them if they'd been inside their living bodies.

This afternoon, however, the sky was a deep serene blue and the sun was still high, blazing down on the snow and shimmering on the thin crust of ice that lay over it like frosting on an already white cake. On many of the trees and bushes, the sun had been warm enough to start melting the snow that lay in swags along branches and twigs, but the breeze had arrested this midday thaw.

On any other occasion, Joe might have enjoyed this walk. But—besides his preoccupation with preparing his story—something else had started to distract his attention. Something that made him feel both confident and uneasy: confident that he was heading in the right direction and uneasy with the consciousness that he might never make it, after all.

He was being watched.

Every step he took was being monitored.

He'd noticed the glances first on the town's outskirts as he walked on the old snow-buried railroad, where it wound its way behind warehouses and factories, schools and private houses. Seemingly casual glances, cast at him through the slats of fences or from the tops of garages. Other ghosts, he decided, who'd noted from his easy progress and lack of footprints that he too was a ghost. Probably—he thought at first—they were just mildly curious, wondering where he was going, then shrugging it off, dismissing him as a nostalgic nut, trying to recapture the pleasures of being out for a country walk on a day like this.

But then Joe began to notice that the glances kept coming even when he'd drawn away from the town, in places where normally no one, living or ghost, would have been lurking—while he was striding out on the low embankment that crossed the fields, on the bridges that had taken the railroad over country roads, past clumps of trees and frozen swamps. Out of the corners of his eyes, he would notice the furtive movements behind bushes or just over the far side of snowdrifts or through the tall rushes. There seemed to be one of these watchers every few hundred yards.

Still he walked on, without changing his pace. But by the time the buildings of Hawkins Station came into view, Joe was so uneasy that he just had to stop and make sure, though without letting them know that he had seen them.

But how?

Had he been a living person, it would have been easy. He'd have simply stopped and pretended to tie his shoelace or blow his nose. But in another ghost, such pretenses would arouse immediate suspicion. Ghosts' shoelaces never came undone; their noses never needed blowing.

It was a ruffed grouse, suddenly arising with a *whir* from under a bush just ahead, that gave Joe his chance. He stopped and pretended to admire the bird's flight. There was nothing suspicious about doing that.

But it gave him the perfect excuse to glance over his shoulder as the grouse whirred past his head. Then, sure enough, he saw a man in a flowery summer shirt waving his arms, crisscross, then darting back behind the trunk of a tree. Joe swiftly turned his head back toward Hawkins Station just in time to see another figure slip around the corner of a shed. That too had to be a ghost. No living woman would be out in a swimsuit in this temperature!

The doctor *must* be here, Joe thought. And I bet he knew I was heading this way a good half hour ago! He thought of the number of Malevs that Purcell must have under his control to organize that kind of bush telegraph. The guy's even more dangerous than I thought, he told himself as he approached the cluster of buildings.

No smoke rose from the chimneys of the steep-roofed station. No light came from any of the boarded-up windows. The deserted parking lot had been plowed, yes, but only as far as the mounds of grit, deposited there by the highway maintenance department.

There was a shed at the side of the main building. Its door had long since rusted off its hinges. But even as Joe drew level with it, moving more slowly now, a figure stepped out.

"OK! Stop right there, b-buddy! What d'ya w-want?"

Muscle—shoulders hunched, jaws twitching.

Joe smiled, pretending to be only slightly surprised.
"I've come to see Dr. Purcell."
Muscle frowned.
"Never heard of him," he said.
"I think you have," said Joe.
The twitching started again, more violently. The gold cross rose and fell on the hairy chest.
"Calling me a l-liar?"
Joe shrugged.
"Sure! Why not? If you *still* say you've never heard of Dr. Purcell."
Muscle took a step forward. His right shoulder came down a couple of inches. Joe braced himself.
"N-nobody c-calls me a l-liar an'—an' gets away with it, fella!"
Muscle took another step toward Joe. Joe was watching those dark glasses now, trying to catch a glimpse of the eyes. Then someone stepped around from the far side of the shed.
"Hold it, Muscle!"
It was the woman in the swimsuit.
Joe didn't dare take his eyes off Muscle's glasses, but he had a quick impression of long blond hair a yellower color than Karen's and a sash with some words on it.
"Huh?"
Muscle turned. Joe relaxed. He took a quick closer look at the woman. The swimsuit was yellow, one-piece. She was well-tanned and wore high-heeled yellow shoes. The words on the sash? *Miss Berkshires 198–.* The rest of the date curved out of sight, behind the slim waist.

"You s-stick around, Mermaid, and watch me b-break this jerk into sm-small pieces!"

The woman's eyes brightened. She had a beaky nose over a pair of thin red lips—and the glitter in her eyes at Muscle's words gave her face a horrible bird-of-prey look.

Then she sighed.

"Sorry, Muscle. Some other time maybe. But can't you read?"

"Huh?"

"On his chest. Armstrong Construction. I've heard Dr. Purcell mention this guy." She gave Joe what was obviously intended to be a friendly smile. "Hi, Mr. Armstrong! Mr. Joseph Armstrong, right?"

Joe forced himself to smile back.

"So *you've* heard of Dr. Purcell," he said.

"Sure!" She shrugged, making the sash rise and fall voluptuously. "Did you come looking for him?"

"Yes," said Joe. Then he gave Muscle a sternly accusing look. "By *invitation!*"

Muscle lowered his head.

"Ya shoulda said!" he mumbled. "C'mon—we'll take ya to him."

Two boards were missing in one of the main building's doors. Mermaid slipped through the gap with much wriggling of the hips.

"Come on," she said, turning to Joe. "It's wider than it looks. Even *he* can do it, if he holds his shoulders sideways."

"Get in!" grunted Muscle, shoving Joe.

Snow had drifted through the gap, but the only prints were a delicate stitchwork made by mice.

The part of the building Joe now found himself in had obviously been the theater's auditorium. There was a small stage to his right, still with some background scenery and a wooden armchair like a rough medieval throne. This chair and its occupant and the attendant figure standing at the side were all in deep shadow. Joe peered at the group, wondering if the figures themselves had been part of the stage property—a couple of waxwork extras—they were so still.

The rest of the auditorium was surprisingly well-lit—mainly by a shaft of sunlight that slanted down from a hole in the roof. Joe was able to see that all the seats had been removed. Now it was just bare boards, thick with mud and dust and what looked like feathers and scattered bones, most of them small and birdlike. A few empty wooden boxes, upturned, a dirty old mattress and scores of empty cans gave evidence of occasional human visitors.

"Not very prepossessing, is it?" said a dry familiar voice.

Joe looked up. His eyes must have quickly adjusted to the general dimness, for now he could see that the speaker, the one in the chair, was Dr. Purcell. The other man—small, neatly dressed in a gray business suit that was the exact color of his hair—still didn't move. The eyes behind his glasses remained fixed on the wall behind Joe, somewhere above his head. This was the man Joe had seen with Purcell before.

Dr. Purcell was staring straight at Joe. The wrinkles around his eyes deepened as the eyes narrowed.

Behind Joe, Muscle stirred.

"The g-guy says you invited him. A-and *she*—she told him you was here. *I* wouldn't have. I was telling him—"

"That's enough, Muscle!" snapped Purcell, still staring at Joe. His face relaxed. "So," he said, "you've decided to pay me a visit at last, eh?"

"Yes, sir."

"Muscle," said Purcell, "you should be downtown, keeping an eye on Maggot."

"Yeah, sure, but—"

"Go, then! Now!"

While this exchange was going on, Joe glanced at the stage backdrop. It represented a stone wall, crusted with moss and festooned with cobwebs. A huge fireplace had been painted in, with blazing logs that even the dust and grime hadn't managed to dim. Also painted on the backdrop, at the side of the fire, was a bench littered with glass condensers and retorts and racks of test tubes. It reminded Joe of Wacko's table—except that this was crowded with the bits and pieces of some chemistry nut rather than a pair of electronics buffs.

"Step up here, please," said Dr. Purcell. "There is a stool here, if it will make you feel better to sit."

The stool was really a footstool. Purcell removed his left foot from it.

"Thanks," said Joe, sitting down. It didn't make him feel better at all, with Purcell looming over him, but if it helped to gain the doctor's confidence, that was OK by Joe.

The other man was still staring off into space.

Mermaid stayed down on the auditorium floor, gazing up at the shaft of light.

"Are you ready to take advantage of my expertise now?" asked Dr. Purcell.

His left leg was crossed over his right. The left foot gave a little kick as he spoke. The shiny brown shoe was only inches away from Joe's face.

But the man's tone had been pleasant enough.

"Yes, sir," said Joe. "I am."

The foot gave another little kick.

"Splendid! You sound as if you've really made up your mind. I like that." Another kick. "I take it that you have now discovered who your murderer was, and can't wait to get your hands—a pair of real *living* hands—on him? Or her? Correct?"

The foot gave a series of mini-kicks. Joe frowned.

"Yes—but—"

The foot went very still.

"Who, may I ask, *was* your killer?"

Joe looked up. The skin on that puckered face looked like the crust on an old, old cheese.

"I'd rather not say, sir. Not at this point."

The plain fact was that Joe still didn't know. And he didn't want to give any name in case Purcell did know.

The crust began to split.

"Of course! We always respect the patient's—uh—the *subject's* privacy in matters of this kind. But"—the

face went still again, the slit mouth barely moved—
"you must be prepared to answer a lot of personal
questions. Concerning yourself only."

"I—such as?"

"My dear young man, if you wish to place yourself
in my hands—well, then!" Dr. Purcell folded those
hands very precisely and gazed down at Joe. "Well,
then, you must look upon me as a clinician, a surgeon.
Like when you were alive. Did you ever undergo surgery?"

"Yes. I had a double hernia when I was nineteen
and—"

"And before your operation you were given a complete work-up?"

"Yes."

"The most important part of which was discussing
the operation with the surgeon?"

"Yes, sir."

Dr. Purcell sat back.

"Well, then—"

"*Dr. Purcell!*"

The doctor scowled. Mermaid was pointing to the
shaft of light, which seemed to have brightened.

Purcell glanced at it, then shook his head. His scowl
cleared.

"Patience, my dear! It isn't ready yet. Memory?"

The gray man was now looking at the shaft.

"At least another ten minutes, sir."

The voice startled Joe. It was very soft, but clear.
It was like a faded imitation of Purcell's own voice.

The doctor must have noted Joe's expression.

"Allow me to introduce you," he said. "My colleague—my most valued colleague—Memory. Memory, this is Joseph Armstrong—"

"Yes, sir. The head of Armstrong Construction, a privately owned company specializing in office building. He died as the result of a fall from one such building under construction, some three years ago. To be precise, at 1:11 on the afternoon of September 6, 19—"

"Yes, Memory," Purcell cut in. "Thank you. There's no need to go through the complete report."

"Report?" said Joe, feeling stunned.

"Yes. The coroner's report. Memory could give you the exact cause of death, pathologically speaking, of course."

"Multiple fractures of the skull," droned the faded voice, "severe damage to the spinal column, a ruptured—"

"Thank you, Memory! Enough!" The foot gave a twirling twitch. "Now, as I was saying, I shall have to ask you a number of personal questions. Purely to ensure that a sufficiently compatible donor is found for you. There's no future in taking over a body that will reject you in the first five minutes, eh?" Dr. Purcell's laugh was like the scuttling of rats' feet over old parchment. "Of course not! So—first—are you left-handed or right-handed?"

"Uh—right-handed."

"Do you—did you, in life—smoke?"

"No."

"Drink alcohol?"

"No."

"Did you use drugs of any kind, illegally?"

"No."

"Are you getting all this down, Memory?"

"Yes, sir," sighed the voice.

Joe glanced up. He was surprised to see no notebook and pen. Then, as he realized that a ghost would never be able to pick up such objects, let alone use them, he heard Purcell's chuckle.

"Yes." It was as if he had read Joe's thoughts. "That's why I've dubbed my colleague Memory. He *is* my memory, in a way. . . . But back to our questions. Did you tend to have to take antacid medication?"

"No, sir."

"Did you find, on the contrary, you needed more acid intake than most people? Citrus fruit? Lemons, especially?"

"Why, yes!"

"As I thought. Most redheads do."

"But—" Joe was genuinely perplexed. "Excuse me, Doctor, but why *these* questions? What do they have to do with—?"

"My dear young man, I couldn't very well give you blood tests and X rays and EEGs. Now *could* I?"

"No, sir, but—"

"But these questions are designed to provide me with just the same kind of clinical information. Your preferences, habits—they all have links with your body chemistry, your genes." Purcell sighed. "Even in life,

I had begun to perfect this method—clinical exploration without instruments—and now the method is indispensable. Shall we proceed?"

"*Dr. Purcell!*"

There was a screech of excitement in Mermaid's voice.

The doctor looked at her sharply, then at the shaft of light. He jumped to his feet.

The shaft looked definitely brighter. Joe guessed that the sun had reached a point in the sky where it had started to shine directly through the hole. The shaft broadened the farther it got from the hole. Right now, it was illuminating part of the floor and several feet up the wall. Mermaid was standing quite near the wall, among the empty cans next to the mattress, fully in the light. She had struck what had probably been her favorite beauty-contest pose: left hand on hip, right hand behind her head, with a smile stretched as wide as her small mean mouth would permit.

"What d'you think?" Dr. Purcell asked Memory.

Memory looked up at the hole, then let his gaze travel slowly along the beam, right down to where Mermaid's yellow shoes shone alongside the empty cans.

"Could you move, very slowly, a few inches forward?" he said, with a tremor of urgency in his voice. "A shade more . . . a shade more . . . *there!* Hold it there!"

Mermaid readjusted her pose. Her eyes flittered hopefully from Memory's face to Dr. Purcell's.

"It looks exactly right to me," Purcell murmured.

88

"You could try it, sir," said Memory. "The intensity seems to be increasing, though. In another few seconds, it could be too strong."

Dr. Purcell nodded. One of the upturned boxes was about six feet in front of Mermaid. He went and stood on it, facing her. Now Purcell too was lighted up from head to foot. If they'd both been in their living bodies, he'd have cast a shadow over the posturing woman, eclipsing her. As it was, he did cast a shadow, but a ghost shadow, a vague, extremely pale gray, a slight dimness that could be seen only by other ghosts.

"Am I positioned correctly, Memory?" he asked, holding himself in a grotesque tweedy mirror image of Mermaid's pose.

"Very slightly—one half inch—no more—to the right, sir?"

The shadow moved fractionally. Every pucker in Purcell's face seemed to be quivering. The slit mouth had vanished in the deepening wrinkles. The eyes had become tiny glittering points.

"*Yes*, Doctor!" Memory whispered harshly.

Mermaid seemed to stiffen. Purcell's shadow—that mere dimness over the brightly illuminated glaring yellows of her hair, her swimsuit and her shoes—began to vibrate.

Joe narrowed his eyes. Purcell was standing as motionless as Mermaid. But yes—there was a definite vibration in his shadow. A very fine vibration—very very fine indeed.

Then it happened.

One second, Joe was watching the vibration, and

the next he saw the woman light up. It was as if a new filter had been placed in the beam, making the top half of Mermaid's body turn an intense whitish blue. He gave Purcell a swift glance, but no difference in color showed there: just the same gray green tweed, the turtle brown face. The only difference was that the eyes had disappeared altogether, lost in the deepened wrinkles.

Then Joe realized that Dr. Purcell was concentrating all his inner powers.

And why?

Dr. Purcell *was* the new filter in that beam! Dr. Purcell had turned himself into a kind of screen!

The upper half of Mermaid glowed with that whitish blue intensity for another two seconds. At one instant, the light seemed to shoot down her right leg, but it quickly faded.

Then Dr. Purcell gave a great gasp and stood down, shaking his head.

"Not quite right yet!" he muttered.

"No, sir." Memory gazed sadly at the now normally illuminated Mermaid. "You came very close, though."

"Relax, girl," said Purcell.

"Aw, but Doc—!"

"I said relax. We'll get it right one of these days."

As Mermaid sat down on one of the boxes, pouting, chin in hands, the picture of disappointment, Purcell turned to Joe.

"I'm sorry," he said. "But this is one of my most important experiments. It can only be conducted at certain times and on certain days. You noticed the difference it made to Mermaid?"

"Yes," said Joe. "A—a kind of brightness?"

Purcell nodded, smiling.

"Well, my dear boy, if you'd been a living person, *you* would have seen that, too!"

Joe stared.

"You mean—you can control the *light?* With—with your micro-energy? Make her *appear?*"

Joe's head was in a spin. He knew that ghosts could sometimes exert such control over their inner energies that they could attract certain extremely small objects. He himself could do it, attracting particles of dust in sunbeams, tiny drops of moisture in mist, even gnats. Karen was good at this, too. And they had both thrown scares into living people by making the shapes of their arms or even their whole bodies appear in such shadowy forms.

But *this!*

There was nothing shadowy about *this!*

This was lighting up a ghost body, showing all its features.

"I've been working on it for years," said Dr. Purcell. "Using my ghost body as a diffraction grating. Producing a superimposed line spectrum on Mermaid's body. . . . Have you noticed something, Memory?"

Memory had been examining his own frail hand in the beam. He nodded.

"Yes, sir. I rather suspect the first-state energy was still greater than E_2."

"Ah!" murmured Purcell. "I had a feeling that might be the case. I must ask you to dig out the notes for Experiment 33(b)."

"Yes, sir." Memory began to stare off into the shadows. "Well, we weren't using natural sunlight then. We were taking advantage of one of the spotlights used in the New Year's cabaret at the Lakeview Hotel. It was—"

"Not *now*, Memory! We'll discuss it later. We don't wish to bore our most welcome guest."

"Oh, you're not boring me, sir!" said Joe, hoping to glean as much information as possible and then submit it to Carlos for *his* expert opinion. "Wow! Boring? No way!"

"Nevertheless," said Purcell, "there's no point in discussing an experiment when it's still far from being successful."

"Not *successful?*" said Joe. "You call that—?"

"No. You saw for yourself. All we can do so far is make the top half of the woman appear." Dr. Purcell gave one of his short rattling laughs. "That's why we *call* her Mermaid.

A loud sob arose from Mermaid.

"But—" Joe began.

"As it is, all *she* would do would be to scare a living person," said Purcell. "Good, I suppose, but not good enough for me. I—"

"Well, it is good enough for *me!*" Mermaid blurted. "All I want to do is pay back that old witch of a foster mother, and she has a weak heart, and even if she saw one-quarter of me, just my head, she'd croak with the shock, and—"

"*That's enough!*" Purcell barked. Mermaid shrank. "No, Joseph," said Purcell, softly and pleasantly. "I want her to appear in full. As a full-size woman. A very *attractive* full-size woman."

Mermaid's frown softened.

Joe stared at Purcell.

"As—as a decoy?"

Purcell laughed and turned to Memory.

"I was right about this young man, you see. Very intelligent." He beamed at Joe. "Oh, but we'll select a very special body for *you!* Now—where were we?"

Joe's head was reeling, thinking how formidable, how dangerous, Purcell must be.

"Ah, yes!" the doctor said. "Now about your aptitudes in school. Did you lean toward the mathematically based subjects or toward—"

He broke off.

The man in the flower shirt had just come in.

"I'm sorry, Doc, but this is urgent!"

Purcell frowned.

"It had better be! You know the rules."

"Yes, sir. Sure! But—I just got word. It's that dope Maggot. He's gotten into a fight again. Some other ghosts, downtown. Straight-type ghosts. Same two as this morning. Plus something about another one—one you'd be personally very interested in. And—and that's all I was told."

12
Another Candidate?

No one invited Joe to tag along when Purcell and Memory hurried off along the railroad track bed, but no one raised any objection, either. Joe was glad. The trouble obviously involved other Ghost Squad members, and he wanted to be on the spot to use whatever influence he had with Dr. Purcell.

When they burst into Santa's grotto, however, it seemed very peaceful.

Tommy Peck was bending to listen to the requests of a very shy little girl. Buzz and Wacko were leaning forward also, trying to catch the kid's words. Maggot was watching Santa rather impatiently while Danny was standing back a little, arms folded, glowering at Buzz.

"What's been going on here?"

Maggot swung around, cringing at the sound of Purcell's voice.

"Sir?"

"I've received word that you'd gotten into another brawl."

Danny had turned, too. His eyes widened when he saw Joe. Luckily, Joe was standing behind Purcell and Memory, and Maggot's scared eyes were fixed on Purcell. Joe ventured a slight shake of the head. Danny seemed to get the message and turned back to his scowling scrutiny of Buzz.

"Well, yes," Maggot said. "I—uh—did have a run-in awhile back. Same two kids as this morning. But Muscle's taking care of them."

Purcell glanced around, frowning.

"How? Where is he?"

"I don't know. He went after him. He told me to mind my own business. Which I am doing, as you can see, sir." Maggot stared at Joe. "Who's he?"

"He's a new candidate," said Purcell. The cold eyes looked Maggot up and down. The slit mouth lifted at one corner in a sneer. "And a precious sight more intelligent than *you!*" Purcell's gaze veered to Danny. "But since we're asking questions—who's *he?*"

Maggot's white tooth flashed in a tentative smirk.

"Oh, him! He's harmless. He's trying to get back at that living kid there. I've been telling him he'll never do it by hitting him. So did Muscle."

Joe stared approvingly at Danny. This was the first he'd heard of the incident, but he realized at once what Danny had really been doing.

Purcell shot Maggot a razor-sharp look.

"Did you tell him that there *were* ways?"

"Well—uh—yes—"

"*What?*"

Maggot backed away.

"But I didn't go into details, Dr. Purcell! Honest! Right, kid?"

Danny looked at Maggot with contempt.

"Yeah. I guess you were just shooting off your mouth." Danny turned to Purcell. "*Was* he, sir? I mean, *he's* been here almost an hour and all he's done is just look at *his* enemy."

Joe felt even prouder of Danny. His young colleague's speech had come out with just the right notes of respect and disbelief.

Maggot was taken in. He winked at Dr. Purcell.

"He thinks I'm aiming to hurt the Santa guy! He doesn't know from—"

"Shut up!" snapped Purcell. He turned to Danny. "Tell me, son," he said softly, "why do you wish to harm the boy there?"

Danny's face began to work convulsively.

"Him?" he almost screamed. "Buzz Phillips? I want to *kill* him!"

Joe groaned inwardly. This time, Danny was overdoing his acting—and placing his friend in great jeopardy. Joe had heard Purcell's sharp intake of breath at Buzz's name.

"So *that's* Buzz Phillips, is it?"

Joe felt it was time to step in.

"*I* know about these two, Dr. Purcell. This one is

Danny Green. He used to be a friend of Phillips. He's sore because—"

"Let the boy tell me himself, thank you, Joseph. . . . Well?"

Between Purcell's cold eyes and Joe's fierce stare, Danny looked flustered. Barely perceptibly, Joe nodded. The gesture was meant to say, OK, you're on your own now! But you better make it sound good!

Danny flushed. Then he put on his angry defiant look.

"Sure I'm sore!" he said. "He—he killed me! At least he was *responsible!*"

"How?" said Purcell mildly—but the one word cut through the atmosphere like a shark's fin suddenly appearing above water.

Danny blinked.

"Well—we were exploring an old factory. The one along River Road that got burned down. We found one of the elevators in the ruins and—and went inside."

Joe was nodding, nodding. . . .

"Then something started to collapse. Thousands of bricks, tons and tons. And *he* shoved me out of his way and dove out to save his own rotten skin!"

Joe had to fight to restrain a smile. That was beautiful, just beautiful. It was so very nearly the truth. The one thing different was that it had actually happened the other way around. It had been Danny who had shoved Buzz. But to safety, thereby sacrificing his own chance of survival.

A few seconds later, Joe felt doubly pleased.

This time Memory took up the tale.

"Yes, sir," he began, "I remember the case. It happened one Sunday afternoon at 3:45, last February. February the twenty-first. His name is, as our friend said, Green. Daniel Green. The boy, Phillips—Robert Phillips, to be precise—gave evidence that this one saved his life by pushing him to safety—"

"The jerk!" Danny snarled. "The dirty, yellow, lying jerk! . . . Oh—you—jerk!"

Danny had begun to swing at Buzz. Again his punches landed just below the nose.

Maggot grinned.

"I keep telling you, kid—"

"And I keep telling *you*," said Purcell. "Shut up!" He turned to Danny. "And you—calm down. . . . Memory, continue, please."

As Memory began to reel off further facts—the precise details of that other coroner's report—Danny gaped at him.

Finally, Purcell turned to Joe.

"You say you know this boy?"

"Slightly. I met him when he first became a ghost. That's when he told me his beef."

"Do you think he might make a suitable candidate?"

Joe frowned. He had to think fast. To have another Ghost Squad member go undercover—and by invitation too—could be very useful. Yet it could also be very dangerous for Danny.

"Well," Joe said slowly, "he's kind of raw—not too bright. . . ."

"But he has the *will!*" murmured Purcell, studying

Danny's scowl as he turned back to Buzz. "He has the thirst to get even."

"Oh, sure!" said Joe. "Otherwise he wouldn't be here, I guess. . . . I'll tell you what—let me sniff around. I'll have some more talks with him, see how really keen he is."

Purcell clapped a hand on Joe's shoulder.

"Splendid! Good idea! . . . Memory, the more I see of Joseph, the more I'm convinced we have a star candidate at last. So intelligent, so—What is the matter?"

Memory had been gazing at the group around Santa.

"I'm sorry, sir, but the other kid—the black one— his face seems very familiar. I've seen him before and—"

Purcell laughed.

"Don't tell me *you* can't remember where!"

Memory's eyes glinted for an instant.

"Of course I can! Sir. It's just that with the foolish hat he's wearing, I was rather sidetracked. That boy, sir, is Henry Williams, the son of the lawyer Sidney Williams."

There was nothing jovial or chaffing about Purcell now. His face was like that of a medieval devil carved in wood that had cracked with the centuries in some dark cathedral crypt.

"Sidney Williams of the state's attorney's office! Yes! *I* can see the resemblance now." The words came out softly, hissing. Then he turned and snapped at Danny: "You! Is that right? Is that other boy's name Williams?"

Danny stared, openmouthed, anxious. His eyes strayed briefly to Joe.

"Yes," said Joe. "I can confirm that, Dr. Purcell."

The man's head seemed to recede into his shoulders as he peered at Wacko.

"Well, well, well . . ." There was a terrible look in his eyes. The slit mouth widened into a grin. "This has been a fortuitous afternoon, Memory. Come along—we have a great deal to discuss. . . . Joseph, we will resume our question-and-answer session tomorrow. Meanwhile, I'd consider it a favor if you'd continue your investigations into the likely candidacy of Green."

Joe was only too glad to comply. He promised to meet Dr. Purcell at Hawkins Station the following afternoon.

When Purcell and Memory had left, Maggot turned to Joe. There was spite as well as curiosity in those hooded eyes.

"So what makes *you* such a star candidate?"

Joe shrugged.

"I don't know. Ask Dr. Purcell. *He* seems to think so."

"Oh, sure! But I wouldn't let it go to your head. He tells them all that. At first."

"You mean he once said it about *you?*" said Joe, sneering, living up to his Malev role.

"Sure!" said Maggot, without seeming to take offense. "Why not? He likes to encourage his new recruits." Then the malicious gleam returned. "But wait until he's got you really hooked into this thing—all programmed, all set up. *Then* you'll see a change!"

Joe wasn't sure he liked the sound of this.

"I don't see what you're—"

"You will!" said Maggot. "Once they've found a donor for you. You'll see *then!*"

"But—"

"Then it'll be, 'Do this! Do that! Don't do this! Don't do that!' And 'Shut up!' . . . You heard him."

"Well"— Joe sounded much cooler than he felt— "when you're so close to going into action, I guess the discipline's necessary."

Surprisingly, Maggot agreed.

"I guess you're right, at that." He looked at Tommy Peck. Tommy was having another swig of cough medicine, between visitors. "Once I get inside that body, I'm gonna be completely dependent on Doc Purcell for—well—what he calls further instructions."

"What further instructions?"

"He doesn't say. But the way I figure it, a guy who can get me into that body and guarantee I'll either survive there or he'll get me out in one piece—he knows what he's doing. He'll be like Mission Control giving instructions to the astronauts."

Danny's eyes were wide.

"It doesn't sound a barrel of fun to *me!*"

"Who's asking *you*, sonny?" sneered Maggot.

"Yeah!" Joe scowled at Danny. "*You* can shut up for starters! Dr. Purcell isn't even sure he wants to offer you the chance."

"Correct!" said Maggot, giving Joe a glance of approval. "It isn't a job for wimps, right, Joseph?"

"Right!" said Joe. He decided to take advantage of this new friendly attitude of Maggot's. "By the way, did you see the way Dr. Purcell looked when he found out the black kid's name?"

Maggot sniggered. "You bet! I wouldn't like to be in *his* shoes! In fact, come to think of it, the Williams kid might be my first assignment, once I get my new body. My first target. Kind of a dummy run, you might say."

Danny gasped. Maggot grinned.

"Sure, wimp! Why not? The doc would love it. Just imagine! Santa strangling one of his own helpers! *Then* I'll get some respect from the boss!"

Danny looked ready to attack Maggot there and then.

"Anyway," Joe said hurriedly, "come on, kid. Let's leave this—uh—astronaut to get on with his observations. You and I'll take a walk, and you can tell me more about yourself."

On the way out, past the fairies, Danny said, "I'm sorry, Joe!"

"What's to be sorry for? You did real good."

"I mean mentioning Buzz's name. It just slipped out and—"

"Forget it! It wasn't as bad as Carlos's boo-boo, mentioning Buzz's astral walking. Anyway, talking about Carlos, we'd better find out what's happened to him and Karen."

"Yeah. They're both pretty fast runners, though."

"That's what I'm counting on."

That and a million other things, Joe was thinking. His head was still reeling from all he'd discovered at Hawkins Station. And now even Wacko had caught the cold calculating attention of the leader of the Prowling Hermits.

It was going to take the Ghost Squad all the luck, courage and expertise they could muster to come out of *this* one unscathed!

13
Carlos Makes a List

Danny's hopes about the safety of Karen and Carlos proved to be well-founded.

"No problem," said Karen, when Joe and Danny finally tracked them down, near Wacko's house. It was getting dark and there was plenty of cover in this neighborhood, with its trees and bushes and hedges. The stars were beginning to pierce the afterglow, and some of the residents had already lighted their Christmas trees and switched on the tiny colored lights festooning their front yards.

Carlos's eyes twinkled like some of the lights as he looked around.

" 'Good King Wenceslas looked out,' " he sang, " 'On the—' "

"Cut it out!" said Joe. "We've been worrying about you."

"Yeah!" grunted Danny. "That guy Muscle looked—"

"Aw, forget him!" said Carlos. "He shoulda been called Muscle-*Bound!*" His eyes flashed. "He didn't have a prayer! Especially on the turns. No speed—no speed at all!"

"Huh! So long as you didn't lead him anywhere near here," muttered Joe as he peered into the shadows.

"No way!" said Karen. "Do you think I'd have allowed it?"

"Hey, Joe!" said Carlos. "Don't look so worried! We just led him a dance downtown, in and out of stores and stuff."

Joe scowled at him. "I'm glad you enjoyed it!" he said. "You know, sometimes I wonder about you, Carlos, when you act like this."

"Like what?" said Carlos, with a cheeky grin.

"Like a kid of nine or ten!"

"Come on, Joe!" said Karen. "I've already told you. We were never in any real danger. Muscle *is* slow. And it *was* kind of fun. And after all, it did take the pressure off Danny."

Joe still looked annoyed.

"You too, huh?" he said to Karen. "Well, wait until you hear *my* report, and we'll see how much fun you think it was *then!*"

"Oh?" Karen was gently biting her lower lip. Carlos's grin had frozen.

"For starters," said Joe, "there might have been more than Muscle to contend with."

"More?" said Karen. "But—" She glanced at Carlos. Carlos shrugged. "We didn't see—"

"You wouldn't have!" said Joe. "Since you were so busy having such great *fun!* But how long d'you think you'd have evaded Muscle if the Purcell bush telegraph had been in operation downtown? Huh?"

"The *what?*" said Karen.

"If there'd been a whole chain of Prowling Hermits," said Joe, "strung along the streets. Signaling to each other. One at every corner, ready to pounce at any time."

"Hey, Joe!" Carlos murmured. "What makes you think they're *that* well organized?"

"My visit to Hawkins Station is what! Luckily for *you*, that's where most of them were—along the old railroad line. Hidden, but watching me, every step of the way."

Then Joe told them about his afternoon's experiences.

Karen's eyes reflected her appreciation of how lucky she and Carlos had been, after all, when Joe was describing his walk. Carlos nodded, too—no longer smiling, but obviously still not shaken. It was only when Joe was telling them about Purcell's experiment with Mermaid that the boy's face lost all traces of high spirits.

"He said *what?*" he kept asking as Joe tried to repeat some of the terms Purcell and Memory had been using. "Are you *sure* he used that word?"

"Positive!" Joe would say. Or: "At least, that's what it sounded like." At one point, he confessed, "I couldn't understand most of it. I was hoping *you* might."

By the time Joe was through describing the experiment, Carlos looked stunned. He'd stopped asking questions. He was now staring off into space, his eyes as dazed and faraway as those of Memory himself.

"Well, I'm glad *something* sobers you up," said Joe.

"Huh?" murmured Carlos.

"He isn't with us anymore," said Karen, smiling. "It's all that scientific stuff. But go on, Joe. What happened next? Did Mermaid seem to *mind* being only half an apparition? Did she look like she'd rather have had the bottom half of her appearing if there *had* to be a choice? I mean, I've seen her around, and she has a face that would stop a locomotive!"

Karen's smile soon faded when Joe went on to describe the scene in Santa's grotto when Memory realized who Wacko was.

"Oh, boy!" she whispered.

Even Carlos snapped out of his reverie.

"Hey, no!" he gasped.

"Yeah," said Danny. "We've got to warn Wacko about that."

"Should we, though?" said Karen. "I mean, you know how nervous he gets."

"Right," said Carlos, frowning. "And that would be one big problem. Especially now."

Joe looked at him.

"Why especially *now*?"

"Well," said Carlos, "after what you just told us,

Wacko's gonna have a lot of heavy work to do in the next few days. Heavy brain work."

"Oh?"

"Sure!" Carlos drawled the word softly. His eyes were glazing over. Then he surfaced once more. "But we can soon warn Wacko if there's any real danger. I mean now that we have *two* undercover agents in the Prowling Hermits, we'll be sure to get an early warning. Right?"

"Well—" Danny didn't look so confident.

"Sure we will," said Joe. "Anyway"—he glanced at Wacko's house—"there's no point in hanging around here tonight."

The others nodded. Wacko had already warned them that he'd be going out to a carol concert with his parents that evening, and that the next meeting would have to be on Sunday morning at 9:30.

"Right," said Danny. "And *I'd* like to look in on Sylvia."

"And I really must see how Dad's coping," said Karen. "He becomes even more depressed near holiday time."

Joe nodded.

"Yes. Sharon does, too," he said, thinking about his wife. . . .

Only Carlos seemed to have no compulsion to visit living relatives. His was a large outgoing family. No danger of depression *there!*

When Joe asked him where he'd be going, he looked up with a start.

"Huh?"

Joe repeated the question. Carlos waved vaguely toward the shadows, the lights, the stars.

"Oh, me—I'll be going for a long, long walk. I have a lot to think about."

Karen turned to Joe.

"I hope we're doing the right thing? Splitting up like this. Tonight."

"What d'you mean?"

"Well—what will the Prowling Hermits be doing?" Karen glanced at Carlos, who seemed to be dreamily contemplating taking his walk along the Milky Way itself. "I mean if Muscle should—"

Joe laughed.

"I wouldn't worry about them too much! Not at this stage. If I know Purcell, they'll all be busy on more important errands than looking for sassy kids."

"Such as?"

"Such as prowling around, looking for likely donors."

When the Ghost Squad met the following morning in Wacko's room, the two living members seemed to be especially cheerful.

"Before we get down to giving each other detailed reports," said Buzz, "we have a news flash. A *good* news flash. Right, Wacko?"

"Right!" said Wacko.

"Let's have it then," said Carlos, through the word processor.

"Well," said Buzz, "it looks like things will be coming to a boil next weekend. Correct?"

Carlos looked at Joe. Joe nodded.

"That's when Tommy will be most vulnerable," he said. "On that sleigh-ride job. Tell him yes—then maybe he'll get to the point."

"*Yes*," Carlos transmitted. "*Very likely things will be coming to a boil next weekend. So?*"

"So," Buzz answered, "it would be useful at that time if we could guarantee round-the-clock twenty-four-hour contact—in here, in our HQ—for the full squad."

The four ghosts looked at each other.

"What's he driving at?" said Karen. "I mean, I guess we could arrange for Carlos to stay here all the time. And we others could come and go, so long as Wacko opened up for us. Even in the night. But where would that leave Buzz?"

"At home in bed," said Joe dryly. "Yet he's talking about the *full* squad."

"Probably he just didn't think about that," said Carlos. Then he transmitted: "*Hey! Buzz! Round-the-clock contact in here just won't be possible. Not for the full squad. You wouldn't be able to be present, for one. Not in the middle of the night, you dope!*"

Buzz laughed.

"Oh, no? *You* tell them, Wacko."

Wacko's grin broadened.

"Sure. Buzz's folks are going to spend Christmas in New Hampshire, with his uncle and aunt. Naturally, Buzz was invited, too."

Buzz nodded. "But that would have been bad news," he said. "It would have left the squad shorthanded, just when we might need every single one of us."

"But it's OK," said Wacko. "He asked permission to stay behind with me, and I fixed it with Mom."

"So I'm going to be a houseguest *here* for Christmas," said Buzz. "Furthermore, Mrs. Williams is going to have another bed put in this room."

"Hey, that's great!" said Carlos, turning to the others.

"Terrific!" said Karen.

"Trust Buzz to think of something like that!" said Danny, gazing at his old friend with admiration.

But Joe was frowning.

"What's wrong, Joe?" asked Karen. "It seems like good news to me."

Joe took a deep breath.

"Oh, sure!" he murmured. "Sure!"

"So?" said Carlos.

"So tell them it *is* good news!" said Joe, a little irritably. "Then maybe we can get on with the main reports!"

While Carlos transmitted his leader's approval, the other ghosts looked at Joe curiously. As Karen said later, weeks afterward, "I could tell that Joe had sensed some kind of snag. Just how big that snag was, though— well—I don't think even he realized it at the time!"

The various reports soon began to divert everyone's attention from this new development, which seemed so minor compared to Joe's account of his visit to Hawkins Station.

And after Carlos had finished telling Buzz and Wacko of Purcell's visit to the grotto, and most of what had gone on under their noses, unseen and unheard by them, they looked totally subdued.

"Whew!" gasped Wacko. "That Purcell guy *really* means business, doesn't he?"

"Danny did well, fooling a guy like that!" murmured Buzz.

"Are you sure we shouldn't tell them about Memory recognizing Wacko?" said Karen.

"No way!" snapped Carlos. "I've told you already— I want Wacko to have a clear head."

"Yeah, and that's about all you *have* told us," said Joe.

But Carlos didn't take the hint.

"Any other message for them?" he asked. "About general plans?"

"Yes," said Joe. "Tell them to keep in touch with Dino and Tommy Peck. To continue as Santa's helpers, in fact."

"It'll have to be after school," said Buzz, when Carlos had passed on Joe's message. "But sure—that's OK by me. Wacko?"

Wacko nodded. "Sure!"

"That's what *you* think!" murmured Carlos, staring hard at Wacko. "There's more important work for *you*, old buddy!"

"What's that supposed to mean?" said Joe.

Carlos shrugged. "I'll be getting to that soon," he said. "Anything else? In general?"

"Yes," said Joe. "Just tell them to proceed with the greatest caution. Even when they don't get a red alert."

Buzz and Wacko nodded firmly when they read this latest warning.

"And what about you guys?" said Buzz. "What will *you* be doing?"

"I'll continue to keep in touch with Dr. Purcell, of course," said Joe.

"Me, too," said Danny.

Joe lifted a hand. Carlos waited. Joe was looking at Danny thoughtfully. Danny's eager smile began to fade—then it bloomed again when Joe said, "Yes, you too—but only when you're invited, Danny. You start pushing, and Purcell will get suspicious. Understood?"

"S-sure! I—uh—but what should I be doing in the meantime?"

"You will be sticking close to Maggot, whenever he visits the grotto. Which should be pretty often."

"Yuck! Lucky you!" Karen turned to Joe. "Anyway, what about me?"

Before Joe could reply, Carlos said, very firmly, "You can help me."

Joe's eyes widened. Karen stared at Carlos.

"How?"

"By covering me," said Carlos. "I'm going to be really busy, and I'll need all my concentration."

He looked very serious.

"For what?" asked Karen.

Carlos didn't reply immediately. He was already busy passing on the information Buzz had asked for.

Only at the end did Karen, Joe and Danny get the answer to the puzzle that Carlos's behavior had been presenting them with.

"As for me—Carlos—" the screen began to declare, *"I'm going to be very busy, mainly here, with Wacko. Doing research work."*

Karen frowned. Joe grunted and stared harder at the screen. Danny blinked and looked at Carlos's dancing, stabbing fingers. Buzz glanced up, surprised.

But Wacko, after going very still for a few seconds, sighed and nodded. He seemed to have guessed what was coming.

"I want you, Wacko, to obtain books, articles, all the material you can get hold of in the next few days, on the following subjects:

> *Doppler effect*
> *Line spectra*
> *Spectral series*
> *Balmer series*
> *Rydberg constants*
> *Planck's Law*
> *Quark theory*
> *Quantum mechanics (any up-to-date studies)"*

Wacko's face brightened with each request. This was an aspect of Carlos he rarely caught a glimpse of nowadays. Because although Carlos *was* a genius, he'd had to work very hard while alive to make that genius count, to transform it into practical achievements. And it had been with the same briskness as this that the living Carlos had hunted up books and articles for the clues and pointers that finally came together in the design of that very word processor. *Then*, of course, Carlos had been able to hunt up the material himself— to pester the librarians and science department staff until he had what he wanted. *Now* he would have to rely entirely on his old partner.

"It'll be a pleasure, Carlos!" said Wacko, looking up from the pad on which he'd been copying the list. "Just like old times!"

"It'll be more than that!" the screen flashed. *"It will probably save lives—yours included. So get started!"*

14
Countdown

The events of the following weekend were so awesome that the days leading up to it seemed comparatively tame. Crowded with incidents—yes. But on the surface, none of those incidents seemed to present anything more threatening than a minor disturbance now and then.

"We just weren't alert *enough!*" Joe said later.

"I know," Karen replied. "But we all had our own special jobs to do. I guess we just concentrated on them *too* closely."

Karen's task wasn't easy in those five or six days after Carlos had transmitted his list. As it turned out, only part of the time was spent in Wacko's room. Much of it was spent in libraries—the public library, the

school's and even the state university extension's—
and it was in these places that Karen had to be at her
most alert. What made it so difficult was the behavior
of the two colleagues she was supposed to be covering.

It was fascinating to watch them. Never had the Ear
Code been used so fast and so frequently. Wacko would
take a book off the shelf and, quick as a mosquito,
Carlos would touch Wacko's right or left ear. If it was
the left, Wacko would put the book back and choose
another. If it was the right, Wacko would instantly
turn to the contents pages and finger each chapter entry
one by one, getting a yes or a no according to whether
Carlos wanted a closer look at that chapter. Sometimes
Wacko would be given two or three rapid yeses. Then
he'd either hurry to the copying machine or put the
book on one side, ready to be taken home. Armfuls of
books were in fact taken back to Wacko's place, with
stacks of copied pages, to be studied at leisure, with
Carlos then using the word processor.

Scientifically, none of it made much sense to Karen.
And after the first fascination had worn off, she might
have found the whole operation boring, if it hadn't
been for her duty to warn Carlos if any Malevs were
around, and especially any Prowling Hermits. Over
the next few days, she was in fact able to give warning
of the approach of several unknown Malevs and, once,
in the university library, a figure she thought she recognized from Joe's description as Memory.

"Uh-oh!" she said. "I think we have a Prowling Hermit!"

"Where?"

Carlos lifted a hand to give Wacko the red alert. Karen grabbed his arm.

"No! Don't! He might see you touching Wacko. Just move away. He's over by the door. I don't think he's focused on anyone yet."

They kept glancing at the newcomer as they wandered around the stacks.

"You *are* talking about the little guy in the gray suit, gray hair?" murmured Carlos.

"Yes. I think it's Memory."

The newcomer was gazing around as if he wasn't quite sure where he was.

"Hm! You could be right," said Carlos, feigning interest in the copying machine.

"I must admit he looks more like a zombie than a Malev," said Karen. "That glassy, dazed look. There's no obvious malice there."

"I wouldn't be so sure." Carlos frowned. "I wonder what information *he's* seeking."

"Maybe Purcell uses him like you're using Wacko. To gather new facts."

Carlos shrugged.

"Maybe. But he'll have to rely on luck. On some stranger happening to open a book or magazine that Purcell's interested in."

The gray ghost seemed to be doing just that—drifting among the desks, peering over the students' shoulders.

"Yes," said Karen. "But whatever *he* sees or hears, he won't have to copy—even if that was possible. From what Joe says, Memory *is* a copying machine, tape recorder and computer, all combined."

Carlos's eyes had a glimmer of envy. "With instant recall—yeah!"

Karen gasped. "Oh, look! He's moving over toward the science stacks! He—he's making straight for Wacko!"

Wacko was looking puzzled. He was taking books off the shelf, staring at the covers, blinking, then putting the books back.

"Maybe we should have given him the red alert, after all!" murmured Carlos.

The gray ghost was standing shoulder to shoulder with Wacko now—glancing curiously at the books' covers.

"If Memory had seen us do that, he *would* have been suspicious!" said Karen.

"Yeah—I know. But let's just hope that Wacko realizes something's wrong. Otherwise . . ."

Carlos frowned. Karen knew exactly what was on his mind. She too was hoping that Wacko wouldn't get restless and whisper something like, "Hey, Carlos! *Are* you interested in this one or *aren't* you?"

Fortunately, a living person—a woman—was also standing quite close to him now, and both Karen and Carlos knew that Wacko would never risk even a whisper so long as the woman remained there.

They were left in suspense for another couple of minutes. Then the gray ghost seemed to lose interest and went to peer over the woman's shoulder instead, to see what book she was leafing through.

"Of course, it might *not* be Memory," said Karen.

"It doesn't matter," said Carlos, slowly. His eyes were very wary. "We'll just have to assume that it *is* Memory. Don't forget—he knows Wacko by sight. We can't afford to show we have any link with him. We'll just have to wait until the guy leaves."

"But that could be hours!" said Karen, watching the gray ghost drift back toward the desks. "Meanwhile, Wacko will really start worrying. And *then* he might start whispering."

But Wacko seemed to sense that something had gone desperately wrong. After browsing for a few minutes longer, he put the last book back on the shelf, yawned, looked at the clock and strolled out. Karen and Carlos followed him at a safe distance until they were sure the gray ghost wasn't following *them*. Then, out in the street, Carlos gave Wacko the red alert sign.

Wacko nodded, rubbing his upper lip. They were passing a supermarket. The strains of "Jingle Bells" came from a loudspeaker, almost drowning Wacko's muttered words: "I guessed as much!"

Carlos brushed his right ear.

"Tell me about it when we get back," Wacko said, quickening his pace.

Carlos did tell him about it, via the word processor. Wacko looked worried when he learned that it could have been Memory at his side.

"Are you going to tell him now about Memory recognizing him?" said Karen.

"Are you kidding?" said Carlos. "We have work to do, remember!"

Then the two science experts got down to their main

task—sifting through the material already gathered—leaving Karen to watch out the window, peering into the deepening shadows down below. She was glad to see no lurking shapes, other than that of a neighbor's cat treading slowly and cautiously in the crusted snow.

As Karen had predicted, Danny's assignment was probably the least pleasant. It wasn't so bad in Santa's grotto late afternoons, when Buzz turned up (Wacko being busy elsewhere, of course). Then Danny didn't feel quite so isolated, even though it was out of the question to attempt to communicate by Ear Code while Maggot was there. And Maggot was there most of the day.

Maggot turned out to be very lazy in his surveillance of Tommy Peck. He put in the time, all right—probably he didn't dare do otherwise. But he didn't work hard. Instead, he passed much of that time chatting with Danny.

At first, Maggot was inclined to be surly and sneering.

"So you think Purcell will make *you* a candidate? Fat chance!"

Danny tried to look indignant.

"Why shouldn't he make me a candidate?" Then, with a flash of his newfound acting prowess, he added, in a less certain tone, "And—and what exactly *is* a candidate, anyway?"

The heavy mustache twitched, the white tooth popped.

"There you go! Too dumb to know *that!* Forget it, dummy! Go play somewhere else!"

Then Danny remembered his main role. He twisted his face into a look of fierce hatred.

"*You* forget it! I'm staying here until that creep Phillips shows!"

Maggot grinned.

"Dummy! Where is he now?"

"In school."

"So why don't you stalk him there?"

Danny lowered his eyes.

"I don't like schools," he muttered. "Never did."

Maggot laughed.

"No, I bet you didn't! Dummy! So go wait some other place. He won't be here before three."

Danny was ready for this. Joe had coached him.

"I—I was thinking maybe if I stuck around with you—I—well—I might pick up some pointers."

Maggot was obviously flattered. A gleam of pleasure lit up those hooded eyes.

"Well, sure you'd pick up some pointers, meathead! If I *let* you."

But he didn't need any further persuading. Probably, as Joe had figured, Maggot was so sneered at and snapped at by Purcell that it came as a refreshing change to dump it on someone else.

So, while the children came visiting Santa, a most peculiar seminar took place in the grotto over the next few days. A Seminar in Slimy Tricks was how Danny himself soon felt about it.

122

"There are all kindsa ways a Malev can get back at living people," Maggot declared, that first session.

Danny pretended to be skeptical.

"Huh! You told me yourself, Saturday, there was *no* way. When I was trying to hurt that creep Phillips. Ghosts just can't hurt living people, you said. So did that big guy—the one with the muscles."

Maggot sneered.

"No way of hurting them by *hitting* them—dope! No."

Then he began to explain.

"You know how some ghosts can attract things, very light things, using their—well—whatever it is? Like magnetism."

"Sure," said Danny. "I've heard of it. Joe Armstrong—"

He stopped. He'd been about to say how he'd seen Joe attract a swarm of gnats and, on one occasion, the floating specks of dust in a sunbeam. But he wasn't supposed to know Joe that well, he reminded himself. Watch it, Danny!

Maggot was looking at him.

"Go on. What about Joe Armstrong?"

"Oh, nothing much! He once told me how he can make fog and smoke and stuff like that—uh—kind of cling to him."

"Him!" jeered Maggot. "Just bragging, I bet. Anyway, some of us can. Maybe even *you* could, if you tried."

Danny shrugged.

123

"So what if I could? How could that help me get back at this creep?"

Buzz had just come on duty.

"Well," said Maggot, "say it's snowing. Not just any old snow. Not sleet and not those hard little pellets like hail—but that very light fluffy stuff."

"Yeah?"

"Well, even if you could only attract the flakes to one small part of your body, like your hand, or your arm below the elbow—" The white tooth emerged in a greasy chuckle. "Why, then you'd be in business!"

Now it was Danny's turn to sneer.

"How? How could I hurt him with *that?* Snowball him to death?"

Maggot's eyes glinted.

"Listen, dummy. Say Phillips is crossing a street. Busy street. Dodging the traffic."

"So?"

"Well, you could suddenly stick that handful of snow in his eyes, couldn't you? Just when he's in the middle of the street. Get it?"

Danny put on a look of awed admiration.

"Gee! You mean—"

"I mean coming out of the blue that handful of snow would catch him way off guard. He wouldn't be able to see for a second or two, and in those two seconds—" The white tooth shone with an evil radiance. "*Bam!* He gets hit by a truck!"

"Wow!" whispered Danny, fighting back an urge to slam his fist into that obscene white tooth.

The next afternoon, Professor Maggot conducted a demonstration.

Every so often, Dino would turn on a concealed fan to change the air. Tommy Peck sometimes grumbled, saying the draft was bad for his chest. But he didn't complain too loudly, seeming always glad of the excuse to take a swig from the flask.

This time, a stronger blast than usual swept through the grotto, making Santa's beard flutter and sending flying the bits of tinsel, dust and shreds of cotton from the fake snow. It lasted only a few seconds, but it gave Maggot his chance.

"There!" he said, pointing to a gossamerlike tuft of cotton. "Can you attract *that*, kid?"

"Well—"

"Try it! Go on!"

Danny lifted his hand to the floating shred. And he really did try, figuring to keep himself on Maggot's good side.

The shred hovered a second or two, arrested in its slow dance. Danny felt genuinely pleased and tried harder—willing the shred to stick to his hand, picturing it doing that as vividly as he could.

It did seem to cling to one of his fingers, but he couldn't be sure until he moved his hand. The shred moved with the finger.

"Good!" said Maggot.

The man's thick husky hateful voice broke Danny's concentration. The shred drifted away, to lodge in Tommy's beard.

"Yeah," said Danny. "But what use would *that* be? An itsy-bitsy piece like that?"

Maggot grinned. "You could kill *him* with that," he said, nodding at Buzz.

"How?"

"Well," said Maggot, "you wouldn't be able to do it *now*, while he's wide awake. But say he's asleep, mouth open, snoring maybe. That's how you could get him. Guide that cotton near his mouth while he's snoring, and he sucks it in—heh! heh! If it goes down the wrong passageway, it could *choke* him."

"Huh!" grunted Danny. "*I* should be so lucky!"

Maggot shrugged.

"I have to admit, it really works best with babies."

Danny looked at him with horror.

"Babies?"

"Yeah!" Maggot's eyelids drooped. He seemed to be relishing what he was picturing. "A ghost I knew once killed his worst enemy's six-month-old kid that way."

Danny suddenly felt sick to his stomach.

And this was the monster who'd been wanting to take over Sylvia's body!

To change the subject, Danny shot him a question he knew would be awkward.

"But isn't taking over some living person's body the best way to kill some other living person?"

Maggot's leer vanished. He glanced uneasily at Tommy Peck.

"Oh, yeah—sure!"

"I mean isn't that what *you're* training for?"

"Yeah." Maggot shot Danny a suspicious glance. "So?"

Danny shrugged.

"Well—I'd always heard it was like suicide. A ghost takes over a living person's body, and he may get to use it to attack somebody with, but he burns out right afterward."

Maggot looked thoughtful, worried, scared and boastful in quick succession.

"Not the way Doc Purcell has it figured. His way, you can go on for years in a living person's body."

"Oh?" said Danny. "So what *is* his way?"

Maggot scowled.

"You ask too many questions, kid," he muttered. "*You'll* never get a shot at it anyway, so you might as well forget it."

Another day, later in the week, it was Maggot who asked the awkward question.

"Tell me something," he said, casually. "That kid, the one with the big *G* on his shirt who was in here Saturday. The one with the blond girl. You know him?"

As soon as Maggot mentioned the *G*, Danny's heart began to sink. Had Maggot noticed some glance, some sign, that betrayed the fact that Danny, Karen and Carlos were partners? But then, if he had, why hadn't he brought the subject up earlier?

Danny decided that an outright denial would be too dangerous. Shrugging, he said, "Oh, him? Sure—his name's Carlos. Carlos Gomez. Used to go to the same school. I didn't know him well, though."

"Huh! So what was he doing in here? Him and the girl? Any idea?"

"Uh—well—sure!" said Danny, thinking fast. "He was a friend of that black kid. Williams."

"Is that so?" murmured Maggot.

Danny felt uneasy.

"Yes. They—they were very close. In fact, they were working on some electronic stuff—TV set or something—when Gomez got electrocuted."

"You don't say!" Maggot's eyes widened. Then he grinned. "Hey, was it the Williams kid's fault that Gomez got fried?"

"No. I don't think so. Why?"

Maggot's grin broadened.

"Maybe *he's* hoping for revenge, too."

"Oh—yeah—well—I wouldn't know," said Danny, conscious that the gleaming eyes were fixed on his own.

Then came a welcome interruption.

There'd been a lull in the visits, and Tommy Peck was taking the opportunity to have a long pull at the flask.

Maggot's eyes switched to the uptilted flask immediately. He moved closer, making sniffing noises.

"Something tells me—" he muttered, before breaking off and stepping back. He looked vexed, baffled.

Danny knew why. He felt like saying, Dummy yourself! Don't you know yet that ghosts have no sense of smell?

But Buzz was no ghost and, quite unwittingly, he came to Maggot's aid.

"Hey, Tommy!" he whispered. "Should you be using that stuff in—"

"Sure!" said Tommy, taking the flask from his lips. "My throat—I told ya before."

"Yeah! But *that's* no cough medicine. I can smell it from here!"

"Yeah, well," mumbled Tommy, rapidly screwing the cap back onto the flask. "It—it's more effective. Uh—used in moderation, of course!"

"Your old enemy's just done me a big favor!" Maggot said, turning to Danny. He looked excited. "In fact, I'd better report this right away."

Yes, thought Danny, watching the leather coat swing around past the corner fairy. And so did I!

He wasn't thinking about the contents of the flask, though. He knew that Buzz would report that. No. Danny was thinking once again about Maggot's interest in Carlos's connection with Wacko.

Was it just ordinary curiosity? Or was there some dangerous idea burrowing away in back of those fleshy eyelids?

Joe's assignment was the most dangerous. As he himself was to confess later, an American agent in World War Two couldn't have been more at risk if he'd been operating in Berlin at Hitler's secret HQ, with the mad dictator's bodyguards lurking in every corner. Joe spent much of his time in the very heart of Prowling Hermit territory, often in the company of Dr. Purcell himself.

The ordeal started at Hawkins Station that first Sunday afternoon. Purcell seemed to be in a brisk clinical mood as he continued with his battery of questions, picking up where he'd left off by asking Joe about his school aptitudes and attainments: subjects he'd liked best; subjects he'd liked least; subjects he'd done well in; subjects in which he'd been below average.

Memory took down all the answers in that invisible mental notebook, occasionally repeating the answer to an earlier question in his eerie Purcell-like voice.

Then the questions turned to more homely matters. What kind of food had Joe liked best? What foods had he disliked? What foods had disagreed with him? Any allergic reactions? How about drinks? Any favorites there? Dislikes? These questions were all asked in the same intense manner. Just as were later questions about Joe's hobbies and other recreational activities.

On the whole, Purcell seemed to be satisfied with the replies. After a couple of hours, he seemed more relaxed, even cheerful.

"Yes, Memory," he said, "I am sure we have a star this time."

"Very possibly, sir," replied Memory.

"Anyway, Joseph," said Purcell, "that's enough for the present. There'll be more questions another day." He sighed. "I'd love to continue now, but even *my* concentration begins to falter after a certain time. So relax. Tell me—have *you* any questions?"

Joe ventured only one.

"Yes, sir. Have you found a donor for me yet?"

Purcell smiled.

"Dear me, no! These things take time. One doesn't even begin that process until all the candidate's details have been evaluated. One can't afford a mismatch, especially with such a superior grade of candidate as yourself."

"I see, sir."

"Do you? Do you really? I think not. . . ." Purcell shook his head slowly. "You must understand, Joseph, that you and, to a *much* lesser degree, Maggot—you will both be the forerunners of a new empire—a new world."

Joe frowned. "Sir?"

"I refer to a world of permanent ghost dwellers in living bodies. Permanent, Joseph! In constant communication with ghosts like myself and Memory. Such dwellers—colonists—will be our direct links with living people of like minds. Even with criminals."

Joe felt himself go tense.

"Criminals? You mean take over *their* bodies?"

"No, no! Don't look so startled, Joseph. I mean the use of—uh—colonists to act as agents between criminals and the ghost world. The more respectable the donor, the better, really."

"But—"

"Think, Joseph! Think! Think what a clever criminal could do if he had the information that ghosts could supply him with." Purcell turned. "Memory—what is that so very apt quotation again?"

" 'I will give thee the treasures of darkness, and hidden riches of secret places. . . .' Isaiah 45: verse 3, sir. In the King James version of the Old Testament."

Purcell gave a thin rusty chuckle.

"Excellent! Precisely!" He turned back. "That, Joseph, is what I shall be able to promise, and deliver, to any of the most powerful criminals on earth. And, in return, such beneficiaries would have to be prepared to do what I—we—require."

"Which they would," Memory said, a wistful look creeping into his eyes.

"Ah, yes!" said Purcell. "Memory knows of that which he speaks, Joseph. He was, when alive, in charge of the computerized bookkeeping of an exceedingly powerful criminal organization, popularly known as the—"

"Sir, you promised never—"

"I'm sorry, Memory! I—ah—get so carried away. . . . But people like that would certainly do what one requires, in return for such treasures and riches. And what one would require"—here, an extremely ugly ripple passed through that network of wrinkles—"would be very much to the liking of such individuals, anyway."

Joe had been thinking with horror of the parallel between Purcell's "colonists" and "communicators" and the Ghost Squad itself. Except that the planted Hermits would be working for the spread of evil and destruction, and would themselves be acting as word processors.

His head began to swim. The painted fire seemed to throb and smolder, the test tubes and vessels to bubble and steam.

"Joseph? Are you all right?"

Purcell was looking at him keenly.

"Sorry, sir! I—you really think it's possible? Your— your plan?"

Purcell smiled.

"The mind boggles, doesn't it? But of course! Why not? You've seen what I've been able to achieve in the field of manifestation. The launching and maintaining of one of us in a living body will be nothing compared to that."

"No, sir. I guess not."

Purcell sighed.

"But first things first. Tomorrow we must continue to concentrate on your work-up tests."

The "work-up" continued the following day with a new line of questioning and probing. This time, Joe was asked in much greater detail than before about his health when alive. Dr. Purcell wanted as complete a list as possible of Joe's illnesses and injuries. Regarding the illnesses, Purcell was especially interested in: any that tended to recur; any that affected the glandular or nervous systems; those that had had any long-standing side effects.

Joe had been generally very fit. Dr. Purcell seemed satisfied with most of the answers—except for one.

"Measles, Memory. Make a careful note of that. It was rather a bad attack, apparently."

The glint appeared fleetingly in the gray eyes.

"I *always* make careful notes of *everything*, sir."

Dr. Purcell frowned, but before he could say anything to Memory, Joe interrupted with, "Is it something serious? Measles?"

"Only when there are certain complications. But you don't appear to have displayed any of the usual signs."

Joe had the impression that Purcell was glad to change the subject and so avoid Memory's vague challenge. Was there some deeply buried hostility between the two Malevs? Was it in fact possible that Purcell was just a smidgen afraid of Memory? Questions of this kind were often running through Joe's head, but he was very careful to keep them strictly to himself.

Purcell was just as thorough in his inquiry into the illnesses of Joe's parents, grandparents and other blood relatives. His expression became very tense when Joe mentioned that an uncle of his father's had suffered from epilepsy. This fact made it necessary for Purcell to check for any possible symptoms in Joe himself, even though no actual illness of this kind had ever been diagnosed.

"Any attack of migraine? . . . Any brief bout of forgetfulness, amnesia? . . . Any spell of giddiness?"

When Joe said he remembered nothing like that, Purcell turned to Memory.

"Anything found at the autopsy? Any brain lesions?"

"None that weren't caused by the fall, sir."

Purcell turned back to Joe.

"You were certainly a very healthy specimen, Joseph." A sly look slid across his face. "You might have lived to be a hale and hearty ninety or more. Doesn't that make you doubly bitter about your murderer?"

Joe didn't have to work hard at looking angry.

"It sure does!"

Purcell smiled. "Don't worry. Your chance will come."
He seemed pleased but exhausted.

"Well," he said, "that's as far as we can take your
examination today. Tomorrow, I shall be able to proceed to a thorough physical checkup."

"*Physical*, sir?"

"Yes, Joseph. Strange as it may seem—a physical.
Or, more precisely—a psycho-physical. Anyway, you'll
see."

The physical was one of the weirdest Joe had ever
undergone. Purcell applied all the noninstrumental tests
that physicians often do apply. He scrutinized Joe's
fingernails, peered at his tongue, pressed a cold dry
finger to each cheek to examine the inside of the eyelids, tapped Joe's chest and back, and made him say,
"Ah!" Each process seemed to take twice as long as
living doctors spent on it, but apparently Purcell was
able to gather much more than twice as much information.

Not that Joe could understand the findings that Purcell kept rapping over his shoulder for Memory to take
note of—obviously in some special code. But it reminded Joe so forcibly of the time he'd been measured
for his wedding suit—with Nick, the tailor, calling out
the measurements to his assistant—that he couldn't
help grinning and remarking on this to Purcell.

Dr. Purcell wasn't amused.

"This is no laughing matter! *Then* you were being
fitted with a suit of cloth. *This* time you're to be fitted
with a suit of living flesh and blood. One false measurement *then*, and the result would have been a mere

135

pinching under the arms or a slackness at the waist. One false measurement *now*, and the result will be— a speedy and probably agonizing death!"

That put a stop to Joe's hilarity.

But not to his own questions. And the one that arose now he felt safe in voicing.

"Does the donor body have to be exactly the same size, sir?"

Purcell clucked impatiently.

"Of course not! I was just going along with your own rather foolish simile. But believe me, certain other factors *do* have to match. . . . Open your mouth, please. I wish to examine your teeth."

During those first days, when he wasn't being examined by Purcell, Joe was expected to continue his probing of Danny. It was mainly, at this stage, a question of Danny's general fitness for the task that interested the leader of the Prowling Hermits.

Was Green really determined enough?

Was he bright enough?

Was he worth taking up the doctor's time in a regular examination?

Joe did his best to feed Purcell with favorable reports without sounding *too* eager.

"You're sure he won't get cold feet?" Purcell asked on Wednesday afternoon.

"Well—you never can be sure of that kind of thing, sir. But—well—pretty sure. Yes."

"And he won't be another Maggot, continually doing stupid things?"

"No, sir. Not as far as I can judge."

"You *are* questioning Green closely enough, aren't you, Joseph?"

"Oh, yes, sir! Not as closely as you could, of course. But I'm doing my best."

(In fact, the only question Joe ever asked Danny at this stage was, "Are you sure you want to go through with this?")

"Hm!" was Purcell's only response to Joe's last reply.

But on Thursday morning, after a long session of questions about Joe's social life—his taste in friends during childhood and as an adult, his relations with neighbors and work associates—Purcell finally came to a decision.

"Bring him in this afternoon, Joseph."

Joe was taken completely by surprise.

"Sir?"

"Green. Bring him in for preliminary questioning."

"By you, sir?"

"Who else? By *Mermaid?*"

"Sorry, sir! Yes. Sure. Here? At Hawkins Station?"

"At the risk of repeating myself—where else?"

"But—but supposing he flunks the preliminary questioning, sir? Would you want him to know so much about your headquarters?"

Purcell grinned. It was very slight, but the tongue tip flicked out, making it the most obscenely evil grin Joe had ever seen, even on *that* face.

Then Purcell gently tapped Joe's chest.

"If Green flunks the preliminary questioning, Joseph," he said slowly, softly, deliberately, "he flunks everything."

"I—I don't quite understand you, sir."

"I mean, Joseph, that he just won't be around to tell anyone what he sees and hears at Hawkins Station. Even as a ghost!"

Joe debated with himself for hours that day. Should he pull Danny out entirely? Or should he level with him and leave it for Danny to decide whether to go through with it?

But even if he did pull Danny out, or Danny himself decided to pull out, wouldn't it be too late now? Wouldn't Dr. Purcell be sure to get suspicious and have Danny brought in for a different kind of questioning—probably backed by some terrible form of torture?

But at least Danny should be warned, Joe decided. And that in itself was dangerous because it would naturally make Danny more nervous than ever. And then he would be at greater risk of flunking the "preliminary questioning." However, there seemed to be nothing else to do, so—having told himself that if push came to shove there was still one more card up his sleeve—Joe went to Dino's.

It was very quiet in the grotto. Buzz hadn't arrived yet, and there were no visitors. Tommy Peck looked morose and jumpy. He kept plucking at the false beard as if it were irritating his skin, casting his bloodshot eyes from time to time on the drinking gnome. Maggot was silent, too, watching Tommy's every twitch. He seemed startled when Joe came up from behind him and told Danny he wanted to speak with him privately.

Then a most peculiar look crossed Maggot's face—part inquisitive, part triumphant—before he turned back to his silent cat-at-a-mousehole scrutiny of Tommy Peck.

"What's with him?" Joe asked on the way out.

"I don't know," said Danny. "He's been kind of quiet all day. I guess he's excited. Or nervous."

"Oh?"

"Yeah. Tommy's been hitting the flask again. And it didn't need anyone to smell the stuff this time. Like Maggot said, 'You can tell by the way he's beginning to slur his words.' "

"Was he? Did *you* notice it?"

"Sure. I know the signs only too well." Danny sighed. "Anyway, I think one of the kids' mothers must have complained because Dino came in a half hour ago and made Tommy hand over the flask."

This would normally have been red-hot news for Joe. But now he heard it in silence—a silence he didn't break until they were standing on the bank of the frozen creek in back of the power plant. It was a quiet spot, even in good weather, but now, with the path under two feet of snow, it was deserted.

"What have we come here for?" said Danny when Joe came to a stop.

"Because it doesn't give any cover for anyone with flapping ears," said Joe.

Then he told Danny about Purcell's invitation.

Danny had become very quiet, very still.

"So there it is, Danny. If you want out now, no one

will blame you. Except—well—it might turn out bad anyway."

Danny nodded. He was gazing into the distance. A school bus had stopped on the hill leading into town, lights flashing. What looked like some multicolored bundles were bouncing off. A black speck was leaping up at one of them. Faint barks of welcome reached the ears of the two ghosts.

"That's OK, Joe," said Danny, in a small thin voice. "I'll go ahead."

"You're sure you—?"

"Sure I'm sure! What kinda creep do you take me for? D'you think I could back out to save my—uh—skin and let Purcell go ahead and maybe start planting jerks like Maggot in the bodies of kids like—like them?"

Joe wanted to clap his hand on Danny's shoulder. But he didn't move or speak.

"Anyway," Danny continued, "like you said—if I back out it'll be sure to make Purcell suspicious, and then they'd really be out to get me. This way I do have a chance." Then, with a flash of annoyance: "What makes you think I might flunk his lousy exam anyway? I'm not dumb, you know! I do know how to act, how to string him along!"

Joe couldn't help smiling—but rather sadly.

"Of course you're not dumb, Danny! But Purcell—well. He's clever—diabolically clever. Anyone could flunk *his* questions."

"Well—*you* haven't, have you?"

"No-o-o," said Joe slowly, thoughtfully.

140

"And you say you might be able to bail me out, even if I do flunk?"

"Well, yes—I think so."

"So what are you worrying about?" said Danny. "Take me to him and let's get it over with!"

Danny's eyes were wide as he trudged over the snow-covered railroad track bed and saw the various scouts and lookouts—less furtive today. And they were wider still when he was taken into the building and saw Purcell and Memory on the stage, with Mermaid, Muscle and Flowery Shirt lounging around in the auditorium—all three looking at him like they were ravenous and he was a prime hamburger.

"Welcome, Daniel!" said Purcell. "And relax, please. You're not entering a lions' den, you know, like your biblical namesake!"

Joe wasn't so sure. There was an atmosphere in there that he hadn't felt before, not even at the start of *his* first visit.

"And don't *you* look so tense, Joseph!" the dry voice floated down. "Daniel isn't *your* responsibility, after all."

Oh, no? Joe thought.

"Anyway," said Purcell, "there's no need for you to be present during my—uh—conversation—with Daniel. Not for any of you, except Memory. So please wait outside. Now! . . . Daniel, kindly step up here."

For Joe, the ordeal of the next half hour was like

waiting in an outer room while someone close was having major surgery. And waiting with unsympathetic strangers, furthermore.

Muscle, Mermaid and Flowery Shirt seemed as if they couldn't care less which way it went. Mermaid did most of the talking out there in the parking lot. Using the piles of grit as pedestals, she struck a series of poses and wondered aloud how long it would take for Purcell to "produce" her full-length.

Only Flowery Shirt seemed interested in her prattle. Muscle ignored her. He looked edgy and kept glancing back at the building—though sometimes Joe caught him taking a sly surly sideways look in his own direction.

Eventually—just as Mermaid was threatening to show them some of the moves she'd learned as a go-go dancer—Danny came out, looking very drawn.

"He says I should wait out here," he told Joe. "He wants to see you."

"How did you—?"

Muscle's bulk came between Joe and Danny. His glasses looked like twin black pits.

"Y-you heard what the kid s-said! G-get in there and don't keep the doc w-waiting!"

Purcell gazed down at Joe in silence for a few seconds. His face and Memory's were in the shadow. Joe was standing in the light from the hole in the roof. It was overcast outside, and Joe was glad that the shaft wasn't as bright as on Saturday.

Then Purcell spoke, softly.

"I fear he might not be all he seems, Joseph."

Joe felt a lurch in his chest. Telling himself to play this cool, he said, "Oh?"

"He seems to have links with the other two. The Gomez boy and the girl," said Purcell, still in a soft tone.

Another lurch. Joe tried to shrug off this question of links.

"Oh, well—sure. He was at school with the Gomez kid. That's a connection—I guess."

"But Memory tells me there was no sign of animosity when he saw them in the library at the same time as Williams. No sign of hostility on the part of Gomez."

Joe had heard about Maggot's theory that Carlos might be sore at Wacko. But he decided to play it dumb. Almost every gently uttered word of Purcell's seemed to conceal a trap—and this might be one of the most dangerous.

"Hostility, sir? As far as I know, they were friends—Gomez and—uh—what'sisname—Williams."

"Hm!" Purcell *seemed* to be buying it. His thoughtful murmur sounded genuine enough, anyway. "I've had some information—not from a terribly reliable source, I must admit—that Gomez might have a grudge against Williams. Apparently, Williams was with him when Gomez was electrocuted."

Joe shook his head.

"I wouldn't know about that, sir."

"No . . . I don't suppose you would. . . . Anyway"—the crispness returned to Purcell's voice—"during my examination of Green, I noticed a great nervousness when the subject of Gomez and Williams and the girl came up."

"Well, he *is* a nervous type."

"I suppose so." Purcell was speaking in a thoughtful manner again. "However, I think we'd better play for safety."

Joe swallowed hard.

"You mean—uh—flunk him?"

The seated figure nodded gravely. There was something exaggerated about the movement, as if Purcell really was playing a part up there. A mocker's part?

"Yes. We have too much at stake. He knows too much already. We must administer the final flunking."

"But—"

"Please ask Muscle to step in here, Joseph," the voice droned on. "Now."

Then Joe knew it was time to play the card he'd had up his sleeve. He only hoped it would be strong enough. He stayed where he was, staring up at the stage.

"Well?" came the voice, harder than before.

Both shadowed heads were bent forward. Purcell and Memory seemed to be gazing at him intently. It was now or never.

"Hey!" said Joe, in an angry yelping tone. *"No!"*

There was dead silence for a couple of seconds.

"No?" came the driest of whispers.

"No!" Joe put on a fierce scowl. "I mean, if what you say is right, the creep's made a fool outa me! Let *me* ice him!"

The seated figure relaxed, sat back, looked up at its companion.

"You *see*, Memory?" Purcell turned back to Joe. "You'd really like that, wouldn't you, Joseph?"

"You bet!" snarled Joe. "Nobody makes a fool outa me! Nobody!"

Another short silence. Then: "All right," said Purcell. "You may have that privilege. But not yet." Joe felt a deep surge of relief. "If the Green creature *is* playing a devious game, I'd like to know why. So, for the present, just continue as usual. Stick close to him, retain his confidence—and find out as much as you can."

"Sure! Yes!" said Joe. "But—the jerk! I—I could—"

"Calm down, Joseph. You're beginning to sound like Muscle! I know how you feel, but just don't let Green see it. Let him think we're still considering his suitability. All right?"

"Yes, sir," said Joe, bowing his head—partly to suggest true Hermitlike submission to the leader's superior wisdom, but mainly to conceal any traces of satisfaction that had crept into his own expression.

It was likely to be a very short-lived satisfaction anyway, if he knew anything about Purcell.

There had been several meetings in Wacko's room over the past few days—mainly to keep a check on each other's progress. None had been so urgent as the one that Thursday evening, however. The extra bed had been fixed up, ready for Buzz's weekend stay, but the ghosts glanced at it without comment. Their chief

145

concern was Danny's narrow escape, which they conveyed immediately, via the screen.

"The big question," said Joe as Buzz and Wacko stared at Carlos's message, "is what made Purcell get so suspicious?"

Carlos transmitted that, too, and promptly supplied the answer.

"That was Joe's question. My own answer would be as follows. Purcell has found out that I'm a friend, or ex-friend, of Wacko's. Also he's found out that Danny was a friend, or ex-friend, of Buzz's. Now obviously Buzz and Wacko are good friends. Purcell and the others will have seen that, when they visited the grotto. So that means both Danny and I— friends or ex-friends of these two surviving friends—must know each other more than just casually. Therefore, *Purcell would realize that Danny was lying when he pretended not to know me very well. Right?"*

"Oh, boy!" Danny murmured. "Right! . . . Hey, I'm sorry, Joe! I—"

"Forget it!" said Joe. "Nice work, Carlos. Now tell them the need for extra-extra caution."

Carlos did that. Buzz and Wacko, both looking worried, nodded. Then Buzz brightened a little.

"There's one thing in our favor, anyway," he said. "They must be even more interested in Tommy Peck just now. It looks like he's ready to cut loose."

Joe, through Carlos and the word processor, said, *"That bad, is it?"*

"The extra swigs from the flask?" said Buzz. "Yeah. But not only that. He was telling me tonight how Dino had bawled him out earlier. And how he, Tommy, was sick of the nagging and was looking forward to the Carmen's Cookery job."

"*So?*"

"So he said he could hardly wait for tomorrow night and the first sleigh ride. Then he'd *prove* that a few drinks can actually make a guy sparkle. His very words."

"Great!" Karen groaned.

"This looks like it, then," said Joe. "We're on countdown."

"Countdown?" said Danny.

"Yeah! To the launching of Tommy's body with Maggot at the controls. It's taking on fuel already, by the sound of it."

"Can't we do anything to save Tommy?" said Karen.

"Like what?" Danny asked. "Snatch the bottle from his hand?"

"Buzz could!" said Karen. "Wacko could!"

"How?" said Joe. "By following him around wherever he goes? Into bars? Into his house? Into Carmen's place? All hours, day and night?" He shook his head. "*We* could, sure! But then *we* can't do much physically to stop him. . . ."

"Couldn't we scare him somehow?" said Karen. "*Scare* him off liquor?"

"What?" said Danny. "By making our hands appear in snowflakes, pointing accusing fingers? Believe me, Karen, alcoholics have much scarier things happen to them—real things—and *still* they go on drinking!"

Karen fell silent.

"I guess we might be able to do something about Maggot," said Carlos, hesitantly. "When the time comes—trip him up—something. . . . No?"

"With all the others around?" said Joe. "This is Purcell's big launching spectacular, remember. All the big shots will be there, plus who knows how many small fry. Any of *us* try to grab Maggot and we'll be torn to shreds. . . . No. We've just got to hope for some technical hitch. . . . Carlos, tell Buzz and Wacko how things stand, but tell *them* to keep a low profile. This is strictly a ghost-versus-ghost matter."

"Low profile, huh?" said Wacko, when he'd read the last message. He glanced at the piles of books and papers—on the table, on the two beds, on the floor. "With all this work still to do, you needn't worry about *me* not keeping a low profile!"

"Me, either!" muttered Buzz, who'd been dragged in for more and more of the legwork during the last couple of days.

Joe turned to Carlos.

"What *are* you working on, anyway? Can't you tell us *yet?*"

"Soon, maybe," Carlos murmured. "It's more advanced than Wacko realizes. Just a few more gaps to fill and . . ." He shrugged. "By the way, when d'you think Purcell might be trying the experiment with Mermaid again?"

"Who knows?" said Joe. "If you ask me, the only thing on his mind right now is Maggot's launching. Plus his suspicions about Danny and you and Karen—and—"

He shook his head.

Karen stared hard at him.

"And who? Not *you*, I hope!"

Joe mustered up a smile.

"A guy like Purcell is suspicious about anybody and everybody. Even about Memory, I would guess." Joe turned to Carlos. "Now let's go over the situation with Buzz and Wacko one more time. It looks like we have one heck of a busy holiday weekend ahead of us."

15
The Launching

Many others in town were beginning to feel the pace heating up, not least the proprietor and staff of Carmen's Cookery. Carmen herself had been so busy with the preparations that she'd had little more than a couple of hours' sleep each night for the past week.

She was a large black-haired, dark-skinned lady. Her father was Spanish, from Madrid, and her mother Moroccan. Carmen had been born in Springfield, Massachusetts, and was as American as apple pie. Deep-dish apple pie was indeed one of the Cookery's specialties, because—although Carmen's menus were renowned for being exotic—she also had a flair for native down-home dishes. Some people said that maybe these were *too* native at times: like her buffalo steaks and squirrel stews and the possum à la queen. And then there were the downright spiteful critics—enemies and rivals—who used to say it was only a matter of time before Carmen served up a special Road-Kill Dinner, in which every item on the menu had been freshly gathered the same day—from the sides of the interstate highway.

But Carmen's imagination didn't stop short at the food. Her place was much grander than the name *Cookery* implied. It had once housed the country club, and it stood at the edge of its own private estate, with wooded walks, bridle paths, a nine-hole golf course, a trout stream and a small lake. This enabled Carmen to serve her exotic food with settings to match. In spring and fall, her medieval dinners would be linked with jousting (on the tennis courts). In summer, she would hire punts for her guests and serve sumptuous French picnic meals on an island in the center of the lake. There were hayrides too, followed by country suppers in the barn, with bluegrass fiddlers and square dancing to follow. And, naturally, in midwinter, there were sleigh rides.

The Christmas sleigh rides were Carmen's pride and joy. Every person who attended her special Christmas dinners had to stay the night in one of the many guest rooms so that there'd be no danger of anyone driving away under the influence of liquor. And this enabled Carmen's imagination really to take flight. The menu and program—printed in the local paper and, of course, much studied by the Ghost Squad in Wacko's room and memorized by Purcell's right-hand man for detailed study at Hawkins Station—said it all.

151

·YE·XMAS·REPAST·

PREDINNER DRINKS, INCLUDING

MULLED CLARET

RUM PUNCH

served in the Armory Lounge,

followed by

DINNER IN THE PANELED BANQUET ROOM

as follows:

VENISON PASTIES FRIAR TUCK

BOAR'S HEAD (WITH ORANGE)

ROAST GOOSE

YE PLUM PUDDING

SERVED WITH APPROPRIATE FINE IMPORTED

WINES, CIDER, MEAD.

Then

·SLEIGH·RIDE·BY·STARLIGHT·WITH·SANTA·

(weather permitting)

to work up an appetite for

MINCE PIES IN THE ARMORY LOUNGE

plus

NIGHTCAPS OF GUESTS' CHOICE

plus

·CHRISTMAS·GHOST·STORIES·BY·FIRELIGHT·

told by Franklin Winterbourne in person,

star of radio & TV

"Does Peck partake of any of this?" Dr. Purcell asked Memory on Friday afternoon. "I mean the food and wine and so on?"

"No, sir," said Memory. "He isn't supposed to show at the Cookery until it's time to pick up the guests. He's rather annoyed about it, in fact."

"Oh?"

"Yes, sir. I think he was hoping to have a free run at the liquor. According to Maggot he was quite angry, saying if the *actor* was allowed to join the guests for the meal, why shouldn't he?"

Purcell smiled.

"Capital!"

For a few seconds, Joe, who'd been asked to join the leading Hermits for the briefing, was puzzled. Memory looked equally baffled.

"Capital, sir?"

"Of course! It will encourage Peck all the more to make his own drinking arrangements. And consequently overdo it. . . . Joseph, I think I can promise you a mind-boggling spectacle tonight!"

"Yes, sir," said Joe, trying to sound enthusiastic.

"Now, as to timing?" said Purcell, turning to Memory.

"The horses will be harnessed nearby, at the Novak farm, around 9:15. Lee Novak will drive them to the Cookery, with Peck up front, dressed as Santa Claus, with the gifts."

"The gifts for the children in the hospital?"

"Yes, sir. The gifts bought by donations from the

Cookery customers and staff. In fact there will be two sack loads each night."

"Very generous," murmured Joe. "They—"

"Quiet, please!" snapped Purcell. "I take it, Memory, that that's because the sleigh has a limited capacity?"

"Yes, sir. It's been built to seat eight. Carmen figures that even though all the guests won't want to go out in the cold, about a dozen will. Which means two journeys per night."

"Excellent!" said Purcell. "With all the more incentive and opportunity for Peck to treat himself to extra drinks. Oh, but we'll see some action tonight, Joseph!"

"Yes," said Memory. "Peck's already gift-wrapped a couple of bottles of bourbon to make them look like regular gifts. One for each sack, so that he can help himself. Maggot watched him do it."

"How is Maggot?"

"Nervous, sir. He too seems to sense that this will be the night."

"Good! So long as the fool doesn't get *too* nervous."

"I think he was a little put out that you hadn't asked him to attend this briefing, sir."

"Pah! He'll have his briefing nearer the time. Then there'll be no danger of his forgetting any of the essential moves. In an operation calling for split-second timing, one can't be too careful."

It was a beautiful night. The temperature was a cold, hard 15 degrees Fahrenheit, but the breeze had dropped and came only in slow fitful puffs. And although there had been a snowfall earlier, it had done no more than cover existing scars and blemishes and restore the overall Christmas-card whiteness to the estate. Overhead, the sky had cleared, fulfilling Carmen's promise of a sleigh ride by starlight.

As they came to the end of the first part of the dinner, the guests looked out with a mixture of satisfaction and anticipation. From where they were sitting, the estate looked like fairyland. Tiny gold and silver lights picked out the minor paths. Larger reds and greens lined the transverse driveway that wound its way from the Cookery to the hospital over on the far side boundary. All that was required now, at 9:25, was for Santa to show.

Carmen was nervously glancing from the clock to the windows. A gentle gust of wind blew some of the freshly fallen snow from the roof in fine sugarlike grains that lit up like sparks as they drifted down through the floodlight beams. "Snowing diamonds," murmured Franklin Winterbourne. "A fitting tribute to our charming hostess!"

"Yeah!" rumbled Carmen, still gazing anxiously at the driveway. "But right now I'd settle for—"

"Santa!" cried one of the guests. "Here he comes!"

Heralded by the chink and tinkle of harness bells, the huge sleigh slid smoothly into view, coming to a stop outside the front door, with the two horses snorting and gently stamping their feet.

"Ho! Ho! Ho!" bellowed the figure in red, next to

the driver, who shot out a steadying hand as Santa stood up, swaying slightly. "All aboard that's comin' aboard!"

The guests' oohs and ahs of admiration would soon have turned to something else had they seen the passengers already aboard, standing on the runners, three on either side. The tall man in the fur hat and leather coat, crouched at Santa's very elbow on the runner nearer the house; the tweedy figure with the reptilian face next to him; the small gray man just behind the second—these three looked sinister enough. But the guests would certainly have felt a chill had they been able to see the three on the far side—so obviously not of this world, as their clothing would have confirmed immediately: the bulky muscular figure in the white sports jacket and open-necked shirt; the other, pleasanter-looking young man in T-shirt and jeans; the weird young woman in high-heeled pumps and bathing suit, who was wearing a big cheesy grin and practicing beauty-contest poses.

Blissfully unaware of the company they were joining, the first six guests—suitably bundled up—came out smiling.

"Hey!" said one of the men. "Why the horses? Where are the reindeer?"

The driver shrugged and grinned bashfully. But Tommy Peck was more than equal to this banter. Tommy was "sparkling" already.

"Ya just ate 'em!" he said. "In the venison pasties! Ho! Ho! Ho!"

Roaring and reeling, he repeated the joke and might

have gone on repeating it indefinitely if Lee Novak hadn't given his cloak a brisk tug, making him sit down heavily.

"Everyone OK?" said Lee, glancing back. "Fine! . . . Giddap!"

It wasn't many seconds before a couple of the guests had struck up with a chorus of "Jingle Bells," and the rest had joined in.

Joe looked back, wondering what all these cozy happy people would have thought if they could see what he could: a rabble of secondary Hermits following on foot, like at a fox hunt, but with the eyes of most of them glowing with something much stronger than a lust for an animal's blood. Joe himself had been privileged to ride with the leaders because, as Purcell had said, "You will probably be the next candidate to be launched, Joseph. So you must study this launching especially carefully."

The sleigh wasn't going fast. Some of the foot followers were managing to keep up with it, loping along at the sides. Flowery Shirt was one of these, and Joe was glad to see that Danny—who'd been granted foot-spectator privileges as a very doubtful possible candidate—wasn't far behind.

Farther back, in the shadows and well away from the rest (Joe hoped), Karen and Carlos would be following the followers. Joe had refused point-blank at first to allow them anywhere near, that night. But Carlos had been so insistent, claiming that it was a vital part of his researches "to see Purcell in action," that Joe had relented.

So, as the sleigh hissed and jingled along under green and red lights, with Santa joining in the singing and the mob raggedly strung out alongside and behind, Purcell took the opportunity to run through the instructions with Maggot yet again—barking them out so that Muscle could hear them, too.

"Remember, make sure there's a ten-foot gap before either of you go into action. At *least* ten feet!"

"That's three strides, right?" said Muscle.

"At least," said Purcell. "Have *you* got that, Maggot?"

Maggot nodded. He was still crouched on the runner, gazing hungrily up into Santa's face. He seemed less nervous now. Just impatient.

Joe wondered if this instruction was really getting through to Maggot, despite the fact that Purcell had gone over it carefully earlier, while the horses were being harnessed.

"So many would-be Hermits make the mistake of attacking the astral body the moment it emerges," Purcell had explained then. "That is why they never last more than a few minutes inside the donor body before they burn out."

This had been news to Joe. He hadn't realized the crucial importance of timing before. But he *had* witnessed the burning out of a possessing ghost only a couple of months earlier. That was when a Malev called Roscoe had knocked out the astral body of a person who had literally been "beside himself" with fury, and then taken immediate possession of the living shell.

Santa suddenly fell silent. The others were still singing. Maggot and his companions watched as Tommy's head drooped. Was the man passing out already? But apparently it was only a ruse. Tommy's left hand was wakeful enough as it slid into one of the sacks and then, equally stealthily, emerged, clutching the gift-wrapped bottle. The package was open at the top. There was a glint of glass as Tommy raised it to his lips, still with his head bent. Then, with a quick jerk, he took a furtive swig.

"Hey-y-y, Tommy!" murmured Lee Novak, reproachfully.

Tommy said nothing. Quickly replacing the bottle, he lifted his head and rejoined the singing, rather more raucously than before.

"Remember also to wait for further instructions, once you're inside," Purcell said to Maggot. "It is always somewhat confusing at first inside a donor body. Everything will seem foggy. But it will pass within seconds. Then you will hear me saying, 'Purcell speaking. Do you hear me?' And you will say, 'Yes, I do hear you.' Just those five words. No more, no fewer. A simple yes will not suffice. Understood?"

Maggot nodded, still gazing at Tommy Peck.

"And don't forget," said Purcell, "I shall be on hand the whole time. You will have nothing to fear, so long as you follow my instructions." Then he barked across at Muscle, "Remember, I want you to knock out the astral body, not kill it!"

Muscle nodded. He was watching Tommy Peck almost as greedily as Maggot.

"Do you hear me?" said Purcell.

"Uh—sure—yes, sir. You told me back at the farm."

That time, Muscle had dared to question Purcell. Looking dismayed, he'd said, "But *why*, Doc? Why can't I just b-break his lousy n-neck?"

"Because I say so!" Purcell had snapped.

Joe was still wondering about this as they approached the hospital. Granted, a ghost knocked out was as conveniently disposed of as a ghost killed—and that went for astral bodies also. The ghost body simply disappeared—instantaneously. It was like those rare occasions when a ghost fell asleep. One moment you would be there—talking, walking, whatever—and the next you'd vanish, leaving no trace, not even for other ghosts to detect. Then, a day or two later, you'd return, finding yourself in exactly the same spot—refreshed, but with your mind a complete blank as to where you'd been.

But why should Purcell be so determined to have Tommy's astral body dealt with in that way? Why not let Muscle simply kill it? Surely Purcell hadn't been affected by the Christmas spirit? Definitely not, thought Joe, catching a glimpse just then of that evil wrinkled face under the first of the hospital floodlights.

As the sleigh drew up alongside the main door, heads appeared in some of the upper windows, and children's voices could be heard, excited in tone but muffled by the double glazing.

"He's here!"

"Hi, Santa!"

"Hooray!"

Then, as Tommy Peck picked up one of the sacks and went, only slightly unsteadily, to the main door, the heads disappeared, and a smiling nurse opened the door and welcomed the visitor—little knowing that she was also admitting Purcell, Maggot, Memory and Muscle.

"Can't we go in?" asked one of the guests.

"No," said Lee Novak. "He won't be long. He's only gonna leave the first bunch of gifts and come straight out. Them's his orders, anyways."

Joe, watching the door, hoped that Lee was right. He knew that Purcell had made allowances for the possibility that Tommy might collapse dead drunk in the hospital itself, making it necessary for the leading Hermits to be on hand. But Joe was as anxious to witness the event as any of the foot followers now crowding around the door, peering in.

"What's going on, Danny?" he called out.

"I think he's being given a cup of coffee," said Danny.

"Let's hope it's laced with rum!" said Flowery Shirt, next to Danny.

"But not *too* well-laced," said Mermaid, who, like Joe, was still standing on the runner of the sleigh. "*We* want to see the launching, too!"

She spoke petulantly, having pleaded in vain to be allowed to go in with the others. "Stay where you are!" Purcell had said. "The more of us go in there, the more some of us are likely to get shut in."

But Tommy took so long at the open door on the way out—shaking the nurse's hand and telling her to have the mistletoe ready for his second visit—that a whole army of ghosts could have marched out without much difficulty.

Having repeated his request several times, Tommy came back to the sleigh and heavily resumed his seat—and the reindeer joke.

"*She* asked me that!" he told the fidgeting guests. " 'Why no reindeer, Santa?' she said. And I said—heh! heh!—you all ate 'em! For dinner! Ho! Ho! Ho!"

One of the guests groaned. Then, as the horses began to trot, Purcell said, "It won't be long now."

"*Was* the coffee laced with rum?" Mermaid asked.

"I don't think so. But it was hardly necessary, anyway. Look!"

Tommy Peck was taking another swig from the gift-wrapped bottle. Nor was it such a very sly swig, this time. The bottle was tilted long and lovingly.

On the second journey, Franklin Winterbourne came along. One of the first bunch of guests had murmured his misgivings to Carmen, saying, "That Santa of yours is really hanging one on tonight!" But Winterbourne had told Carmen not to worry.

"I'm an actor, remember," he'd said. "I'm more than equal to taking over his part if he should pass out."

Purcell had been amused at the irony of this.

"That makes *two* ready to take over," he said as the driver picked up the reins.

But Maggot was far too tense to enjoy the joke.

"Him I don't like!" he snarled, glaring at Winterbourne as if the actor were indeed a serious rival.

"Just concentrate on Peck!" snapped Purcell.

Tommy was reaching into the second sack—the full one. There was absolutely no stealth in his movements now as he clawed at the wrappings.

"That's the second bottle," said Muscle, grinning, as Tommy unscrewed the cap. "Oh, boy! G-go, man, go!"

Lee Novak was not so pleased.

"Hey, Tommy! Don't you think you've had enough?"

"Ah, shut up, Lee!" growled Tommy, removing the bottle from his mouth so clumsily that some of the contents slurped into his beard. "See wh' cha made me do? Ya—ya gettin' on my nerves!" He took another swig. "Ya beginnin' to sound like—like that dumb Dino. Heh, heh! Dumb Dino, Dumdino, Dumdino, Dum—"

As Tommy began to make this into a tuneless song, he suddenly lurched sideways. He would certainly have fallen off if Lee hadn't grabbed his arm.

Still clutching at Tommy, Lee stopped the horses. "You OK?" he said.

Tommy didn't reply. His eyes were open, but glazed—one reflecting a green light, the other a red. His lips were moving, but soundlessly.

"Maybe we'd better turn back," murmured one of the guests.

Dr. Purcell, who had been bending close to the sick man's face, turned to Maggot and waved for Muscle to come over to that side.

"Now," he said, "to your stations—and remember the drill. When his astral body walks, you accompany it closely, Muscle. You, Maggot, remain at the side of the parent body. And on no account do anything until there's a ten-foot gap between the two. *Either* of you!"

Lee Novak was now edging out of his own seat to allow Tommy to slump sideways.

"Is one of you's a doctor?" he asked, in a low frightened voice.

The passengers looked at each other, shaking their heads. Joe couldn't help smiling grimly. The only doctor present was already in attendance, bending closer!

Tommy's breathing was harsh, snorelike, but his eyes were still open.

Purcell lifted his left hand and held it poised above his head.

One of the passengers said, "I think we'd better get him back to the hospital."

"Maybe," said Lee Novak. "But—"

"Better not move him now," said one of the younger men. "Why don't I run to the hospital and get help?"

Lee nodded. "Go ahead!" he murmured. He reached out, intending to remove the beard. But just then, Tommy Peck's body gave a violent twitch.

"Is—is he going into convulsions?" a woman asked.

But the twitch wasn't followed by any others. Tommy seemed to lapse into a deeper coma, half closing his eyes, still showing red and green reflections.

And that was when his astral body emerged.

At first, Joe thought he was seeing double as the ghostly body slid sideways alongside the parent body.

"Wait! Wait!" growled Purcell, his right hand gripping Maggot's shoulder.

Then, as the astral body rose, leaving its counterpart still sprawling on the front seats, gasps escaped from some of the ghostly bystanders. One of these was Joe. He just hadn't foreseen that Tommy Peck's astral body would take off in the Santa costume, complete with whiskers! But of course it figured. Like the ghosts of astral dreamers and delirious sick people—who usually wore pajamas or nightdresses—other temporary ghosts wore whatever *their* parent bodies happened to be wearing at the time.

The ghost spectators fell silent as this phantom figure of Santa Claus slowly looked around, then stepped down off the sleigh and began to walk.

"Watch it!" Purcell commanded Maggot, gripping his shoulder tighter. "Watch the *astral* body! Count the paces!"

Maggot, with an effort, turned from the slumped figure on the seats.

The astral counterpart stopped after two paces and stared at the sleigh. It stroked its beard thoughtfully, seeming to hesitate.

"Next to him, Muscle! Get *next* to him! Close up!"

Purcell was conducting this eerie ballet with both hands now.

Muscle nodded, jaw muscles twitching as he went and stood shoulder to shoulder with the astral body. The temporary ghost gave the real one a brief curious glance, but then turned its gaze back to the parent body, as if fascinated by it.

Then the astral Santa shrugged, turned away and slowly began to step forward in the direction of the Cookery's lights.

"Get ready, Muscle! Knock out only, remember! . . . *Now!*"

Muscle gave the astral body a crisp professional chop to the side of the head. The astral Santa sagged at the knees—then vanished.

Joe winced, wondering what the kids back at the hospital would have thought if they'd witnessed this—this what? This mugging? Yeah! The mugging of Santa Claus!

"Good," Joe heard Purcell murmur. "Now—"

But Purcell was too late. When he turned to where Maggot had been crouching, he saw—nothing.

All the other ghosts had been watching Muscle. None of them—Joe and Purcell included—had seen Maggot merge with Tommy Peck.

"Where—?" Mermaid began.

In answer, Tommy's body began to stir. The glazed eyes blinked.

"Purcell speaking," rasped the leader's voice, "do you hear me?"

The passengers too were watching Tommy. All *they* could see was that this dead-drunk person had suddenly recovered and was looking around with what seemed like cold sobriety—cold and slightly malignant.

"Purcell speaking"—the rasp was repeated—"do you hear me?"

The cold eyes blinked, then glazed over again slightly.

"Yes—I—I do hear you"—the voice was thick, husky, strangely unlike Tommy Peck's normal voice—"I hear you, Dr. Purcell."

Once again, the passengers looked at each other and frowned. To them, hearing only the sick man's side of the exchange, those last words sounded especially creepy.

"Steady!" hissed Purcell.

"He's hallucinating!" whispered Franklin Winterbourne.

The malignancy had returned to Tommy's eyes. They came to rest on the actor. The hatred in them increased.

"And *you*—you I definitely do not like!"

The husky voice now had a snarling undertone.

"Stay down, Maggot!" urged Purcell. "Stay! You're still getting Peck's after-signals. Wait until the electromagnetic fog clears!"

But the body of Tommy Peck was bending forward, reaching out, making a slow-motion grab at Franklin Winterbourne's throat, the fingers like cramped feelers.

"Take *me* over, huh? You'd take *me* over, would you—wimp?"

The words came in that same husky snarl, the reaching fingers flexing in time.

"Oh, you *idiot!*" shrieked Purcell.

He'd seen those fingers suddenly stiffen and a shudder go through the body. He watched, his face twisted with fury as the body slumped back, its mouth working—mumbling and murmuring incoherently—with only the hatred in the tone being communicated to the bystanders, and even that fading, fading. . . .

Then another voice droned out, behind Purcell.

" 'And thou shalt be brought down, and shalt speak out of the ground, and thy speech shall be low out of the dust, and thy voice shall be, as of one that hath a familiar spirit, out of the ground, and thy speech shall whisper out of the dust.' Isaiah, chapter 29: verse 4. From the—"

"Shut up!" snarled Purcell.

"Sorry, sir," said Memory. "I couldn't help—"

"I said shut up!" Purcell swung back to the body. "Maybe with a little luck—"

He broke off.

Yet again it seemed that Tommy Peck was yielding up an astral body—a second astral body. But this one was dark, almost black, charred from top to bottom, with only the vague cracked and creased outlines of the fur hat and long leather coat discernible. And yet it could move, sliding out of the other body slowly, painfully. It made one effort to stand but got no farther than its knees before rolling headlong into the snow, where it instantly collapsed in a heap of ashes.

Joe had seen this happen before, with the burnout of Roscoe, but it still made him feel sick as he stared at the spot where the ashes were shrinking, where they dwindled and disappeared—all in a matter of seconds.

Then there was nothing. No melted snow. Not even a smudge on the smooth white surface.

Murmurs began to rise all around. The Hermits were staring at Purcell now, awed but with their disappointment rapidly increasing.

"The fool!" Purcell cried. He was so furious, so blazing mad, that the nearest of his followers hurriedly backed away. "The fool!" Purcell screamed again. "He couldn't wait! He just *had* to attack at random, within seconds!" The murmurs rose again, angry this time, angry in sympathy with the leader. "The fool, the fool! He probably didn't wait until the astral body was far enough away. . . . *Did* he, Memory?"

"I'm afraid I wasn't watching, sir. I was—"

"Fools! All of you! This is what comes of not obeying my instructions to the letter. Take note of that! All of you!"

The watchers backed away farther, heads bent, eyes averted. . . .

Meanwhile, Lee Novak had started to look panicky. The last sounds that Tommy Peck had uttered had been scary enough, but now—

"He's—has he croaked?" Lee whispered.

Tommy was lying very still. Someone reached under the beard.

"No. There's a pulse. He's gone into a coma. Where on earth is the help that—oh! Thank goodness! The ambulance is here!"

Franklin Winterbourne looked spooked and worried as Tommy Peck was eased onto the stretcher. The actor made no attempt to keep his promise to Carmen.

He seemed to be reflecting that this was an act that was going to be extraordinarily hard to follow. If indeed it didn't turn out to be a showstopper.

But the show hadn't stopped for the Ghost Squad— as Joe was very soon to find out.

16
Dr. Purcell's Bombshell

After the ambulance and sleigh had gone, Dr. Purcell held his inquest on the spot. Only the inner circle of Hermits and Joe were allowed to remain. Some of the foot followers, including Danny, were still lurking in the shadows, out of earshot. Any attempt on their part to creep closer was met with a sharp piercing look from Purcell, and that was enough to send them scurrying back. His face was such a tightly puckered picture of fury, outrage, bitterness and lust for punishing someone, anyone, that his gaze must have seemed to many of the followers to be capable of reducing *them* to ashes.

Memory was the first to be censured.

"You should have noted exactly when Maggot began

171

to take possession," Purcell told him. "In relation to the distance the astral body had covered."

Memory's head was bowed. Joe noticed that his eyes had suddenly closed, and his shoulders stiffened at Purcell's first words.

"Yes, sir."

The voice was barely audible.

"There is nothing you could have done to prevent the fool from being so precipitate, I know," Purcell continued. "But it would have been useful for the record. Even failures can be turned into successes—if they are recorded with meticulous accuracy."

"Of course, sir," whispered Memory.

His eyes were still shut, his head still bowed. Was it shame, Joe wondered. Or was there a deep vein of hatred slowly beginning to leak and seep through Memory's system?

"And Muscle," Purcell said, his mouth snapping, "you are not entirely without blame yourself."

Muscle quivered and twitched.

"*Me?* I—*I* didn't do nothing wrong! I waited until more than th-three paces! I knocked him ou-out instead of wasting him! J-just like you said! I—"

"But you failed to report accurately on just how overeager and therefore unstable Maggot was becoming in those last hours."

Muscle scowled—but at Purcell's shoes, not his face.

"He was a jerk," he mumbled. "How was—?"

"That's enough! We are all to blame in some measure." Purcell paused. "Even I."

"*You*, Doc?" whispered Mermaid.

172

"Yes. I failed to take into account Peck's hostility toward Winterbourne—his resentment of the actor's being allowed to eat and drink with the guests. You look surprised, Joseph."

"Well—uh—puzzled, sir. I mean, what difference would that make? To Maggot?"

"A good question." Purcell seemed to be recovering his composure. Behind him, the moon was slowly rising beyond the trees. "Singularly good, coming from another candidate. . . . The difference a donor's state of mind can make is negligible—if the possessor observes the rules. But it can influence the possessor if he rushes in before allowing the donor's feelings and the signals generated by them to fade. Understand?"

"You think Maggot picked up on some of Tommy's attitude—"

"Precisely, Joseph! Particularly since he himself had taken a dislike to Winterbourne, quite independently. But with the two attitudes coinciding—donor's and possessor's—it was enough to trigger the fatal attack. Fatal to the possessor."

The others stood in silence, waiting for Purcell's next words. He seemed to be deep in thought. Then he shrugged.

"Anyway, perhaps you can all see now why I ordered Peck's astral body to be knocked out rather than killed. Without it, and without any other form of possession, Peck himself would die within a week or so. Now, as things are, he can have his astral body back, and we can try to use him later—more successfully."

Purcell suddenly grinned, ferociously.

"No, Joseph! Don't look so worried! He wouldn't make a good donor for you. For *you* we will find somebody special. Very special. In fact—" Purcell paused. His grin broadened, but lost its ferocity. It was now more of a leer. "In fact—we *have!*"

"Already, sir? Found a donor for *me?*"

"Yes—the boy, Robert Phillips."

Joe was stunned. He'd always had the uneasy feeling that Buzz might one day be selected by the Hermits as a donor. That was why he'd regarded the Christmas weekend sleeping arrangements as a possible snag—with Buzz attracting Purcell's attention directly to the Ghost Squad's headquarters. But he never for one moment imagined that he himself would be chosen to do the taking over!

"Buzz—uh—Robert Phillips?"

"Yes," murmured Purcell, his eyes fixed on Joe's face. "Buzz *is* the name he goes by. I suppose you've heard Green mention him quite a lot?"

"Sure—yes, sir."

"Which makes me glad I decided to delay Green's execution. You should be able to find out much more about Phillips from him."

Joe glanced around. Mermaid seemed as surprised as he was. Even Muscle was looking perplexed. Memory, however, was nodding in agreement.

"Sure!" Joe said, hoping he sounded sufficiently gung ho.

"More importantly, however, I want you to find out more about Phillips—from Phillips."

"Sir?"

"Naturally. To study him, Joseph, in all his movements, at all hours, especially at night. That is his weakness—his habit of astral dreaming. Find out the conditions that cause him to dream that way—what he eats for supper, which side he sleeps on, and so on."

Joe was now able to put more conviction into his acting.

"I'll do that!" he said, enthusiastically. "I think I know where he lives. Green once mentioned—"

"No." Purcell shook his head. "In the next few days you won't find him at his usual address. His family is going away for Christmas."

Joe blinked. This was almost as big a shock as the first. How did Purcell know about *that?*

"But don't look so disappointed. Phillips himself isn't going far. *He'll* be spending Christmas at his friend Henry Williams's house."

Joe choked back a gasp of astonishment.

"Are—are you sure, sir?"

"Of course I am! Memory has spent quite some time researching Phillips's medical history, this past week or so."

Joe stole a quick glance at Memory. The gray ghost was staring into space.

"That is right, is it not, Memory?" said Purcell.

"It is, sir."

"With his customary diligence—"

"Thank you, sir."

"Memory has been picking up vital facts and statistics concerning Phillips at the family physician's office. Also at the hospital—where Phillips spent some time after the factory accident, you know. And, of course, in the Phillips house. That's where he learned of the donor's Christmas movements."

"I see, sir," said Joe, wondering what else Memory had found out. "Anyway, I'll try and get into the Williams house as soon as possible. Maybe sleeping in a strange bed will make the kid more likely to have his astral dreams."

Purcell looked pleased.

"Excellent, Joseph! I knew *you* wouldn't let me down! I knew you'd show far more intelligence than"—he glanced sourly at the spot where Maggot's last remains had shriveled to nothing—"than *that* thing! In fact," he said, looking up, "I'm counting on you now." He lowered his voice. "After tonight's fiasco, my authority is in danger of being eroded. My followers could start to lose confidence. That is why I need to arrange another launching—a successful one, this time—as soon as possible."

"You bet!" said Joe.

"And don't forget," said Purcell, his eyes gleaming, "as well as a donor, you will also have a target."

Joe stared. Were these shock waves *never* going to stop?

"Target?"

"Yes. The Williams brat. Once you've taken over Phillips's body, you will be able to kill Williams. Making it look like an accident, of course. Phillips is obviously accident-prone. After all, he was with Green when *he* was killed. Correct?"

"Uh—yeah—yes, sir."

"I see you are overwhelmed with delight at the prospect, Joseph. And no wonder, when one considers what excellent practice it will be for when you go after your own murderer!"

17
"I've Got It, I've Got It!"

Buzz and Wacko were stunned the following morning, when they heard about Dr. Purcell's bombshell. Buzz had only just moved in for the weekend; his bag was still lying unpacked on the spare bed. He had been flushed—partly because of the excitement of the visit itself and partly because of the news that had already started to spread.

"Hey, you guys!" he had said, even before Carlos had finished announcing the presence of all four ghosts, "what happened with Tommy? Is it true he's in a coma after falling dead drunk off the sleigh? Does that mean Maggot didn't make it? I mean, come on! What happened? Huh?"

Carlos looked at Joe.

"What do I tell him? Do I get straight to the part that concerns *him?*"

"Better break it gently," said Joe. "Tell them what happened to Tommy and Maggot first."

Carlos did this. Buzz and Wacko watched the screen spellbound as the grisly account of Maggot's burnout was unfolded. But when it came to the news of Purcell's new plan, both living boys spun around in their chairs.

"What?" gasped Buzz. "Me? A—a donor?"

"*Sorry!*" came the reply. "*But that's what he told Joe.*"

Buzz gaped at the screen.

"Oh, boy!" he murmured. "Oh, boy!" Then he turned. "But"—he forced a smile—"thank goodness he picked *you* as—as the candidate, Joe!"

"Tell him yes," said Joe. "But not to relax *too* much. When Purcell finds out I've no intention of going through with it, he'll simply pick another Hermit for the job."

After Carlos had relayed that message, Wacko frowned.

"He's right, Buzz. What we all have to do now is stop Purcell. Period. . . . Carlos, how far off are we from putting *your* plan into action?"

The other ghosts looked at Carlos. This was the first real confirmation they'd had that there *was* a definite plan behind his researches.

Carlos looked harassed.

"*It depends,*" he transmitted. "*You know that as well as I do, Wacko. It could be days, weeks. It all depends.*"

"On what, for Pete's sake?" said Karen.

"Be quiet!" said Joe. "Whatever your plan is, Carlos, even a few days may be too late."

Wacko himself seemed to realize the pointlessness of continuing along that line. His eyes narrowed as he changed the subject and said, "There's one thing that doesn't seem to make sense."

"*What's that?*" Carlos asked.

"I'm thinking about Purcell's painstaking matching system," said Wacko. "How could Memory get enough details about Buzz's medical background in just under a week?"

"Yeah!" said Buzz. "Memory couldn't just riffle through the files like a living person. From what you guys have said before, it takes months."

Joe sighed.

"Yes," he said. "I've been thinking about that myself. Maybe Memory hasn't gathered any information about Buzz at all."

"You think it's all baloney?" said Danny. "All that stuff about matching up donors and Hermits? All those questions?"

"No," Joe said thoughtfully. "I'm sure Memory found out all he needed about Tommy Peck, for instance."

"But it would take months!" said Danny. "Like Buzz has just said."

"It probably did," said Joe. "That's why Purcell didn't want Tommy to die if Maggot failed. He wouldn't want all that research wasted."

"Shall I tell *them* all this?" asked Carlos, glancing at Buzz and Wacko.

"Sure," said Joe. "From now on, we have to share everything we know. *Everything*," he added, with a meaning look. "Including your—uh—plan."

Carlos nodded.

"OK," he murmured. "But let me just get this across first."

He transmitted the fact that in Joe's opinion a week probably wasn't anything like long enough for Memory to have collected enough details about Buzz.

"So?" said Buzz.

"So either Purcell is prepared to take months over *this*," said Joe. "In which case there's no great urgency as far as we're concerned. Or"—he paused—"or he wants it done soon and just isn't bothered whether it's a long-term success or not."

"But why—"

"Just tell them that first, Carlos."

When Carlos had passed on this message, Buzz himself took up the question.

"But why shouldn't he want it to be a success?"

Joe's reply soon followed, via Carlos.

"He'll want it to be a success, all right, but not necessarily a long-term one. Joe believes that Purcell wants him to take over your body and then burn out in an immediate suicide attack." There was a pause. *"On you, Wacko."*

"What?"

This time the word exploded from Wacko's mouth. Buzz looked shocked. So did Karen. She'd heard this earlier, when the ghosts had met up outside Wacko's house, but she still found it hard to take.

"But—do you *really* think that, Joe?" she said. "I mean—you're supposed to be Purcell's star candidate."

"I *was*," said Joe. "But now I believe he's definitely suspicious about me as well as Danny. If I refuse to go ahead, he'll know for sure I'm not the Malev I'm supposed to be. Even if I did go ahead, he'd still have doubts—thinking maybe I was only going along with the assignment to save my own skin. So—sure—why should he worry about me burning out? Especially if it takes out Wacko and Buzz at the same time."

After Carlos had transmitted this, Wacko said, "But that means he must have found out about Joe's links with us. Maybe about the Ghost Squad itself!" His eyes were anxious as he cast swift glances around the room. "Do—do you think one of them managed to get in here?"

"No way!" came the reply. *"We'd have been sure to spot any intruder like that. Anyway, Purcell wouldn't need to have a spy in here for his suspicions to be aroused. He's a doctor, remember. And doctors are trained to pick up on slips of the tongue, indirect clues, things like that. Plus he's got Memory around him, making like a computer. No—I say he probably picked up on something very slight and put two and two together—the way he got suspicious about Danny."*

Joe was nodding. "That's just about it, Carlos," he said. "It can't have been anything definite, otherwise there wouldn't be any need for a test. But—"

"Anyway," said Buzz, "what do we do *now?*"

"I suppose the others could make sure none of the

Hermits get near you while you're asleep," said Wacko, doubtfully.

"Oh, sure!" said Buzz. "For the rest of my life, huh?" He groaned. "Maybe I should try not to sleep anymore—ever!"

Wacko winced.

"No. Well—Joe will just have to stall him for a while."

"Yeah, but how?" said Buzz.

Wacko shrugged. "Maybe the others have already thought of something—?" He turned, a hopeful look creeping into his eyes.

The ghosts looked at each other.

They had discussed this in the early hours and had decided that stalling wouldn't be much good. Purcell would soon get impatient and select another candidate—after dealing with Joe either as a failure or, worse still, a spy.

"I guess we'll have to admit we're just as stumped as they are," said Joe.

"I'd been hoping one of *them* might come up with an idea," said Karen.

"So we'd better tell them—"

Joe broke off, staring at Carlos.

Instead of just his fingers dancing, Carlos's whole body was now doing a jig, hopping from foot to foot, turning this way and that, his eyes darting from one corner of the room to another.

"I've got it, I've got it!" he sang. "That's exactly what we need!"

"Huh?" Danny was gaping at him.

Karen looked scared.

Joe was watching Carlos narrowly, trying to follow the direction of his glances.

"*What's* exactly what we need?" he said.

Carlos's gyrating stopped. He turned to the keyboard and transmitted his answer for the whole squad to read.

"*What we need are some decent Christmas decorations in here!*"

Wacko turned. "Have you flipped?" he gasped. Then: "Hey! Guys! *Has* he?"

The reply came back promptly.

"*Of course I haven't! Pay attention! All of you! Especially you, Wacko!*"

It was as well that Carlos gave that preliminary caution. Because although the others did pay attention, much of what Carlos transmitted next was way over their heads. Wacko, however, after stiffening, soon began nodding rapidly. Finally, he began to enthuse.

"Oh, boy! If only you can pull it off, Carlos! I mean right here, in this room, instead of waiting until—"

"*Sure I can! You should know that! These last few days I never worked so hard in my—in either of my lives! So of course I can pull it off! So long as you get started right away and set it up correctly!*"

18
Final
Preparations

By 5:30 that afternoon, Wacko's room had been transformed. Not only had Buzz's things been stowed away, but the table had been cleared of its jumble of spare parts, tools, instruments and circuit diagrams, leaving only the word processor in its usual place. It was no longer the focal point of the room, however. *That* position of honor had been taken over by a Christmas tree, set up in a corner next to the table.

The tree was fairly small, but it loomed large in that room. It had been decorated with dozens of small glass ornaments—crimson partridges, golden pears, silver stars, electric-blue fishes—all jostling for space in what looked more like a tinsel waterfall than a tree. And as if all that weren't showy enough, there was a plastic group set at the foot of it: the three Wise Men, complete with camels—a group almost as coarse in its coloring as Dino's garden gnomes.

In fact the decorations had been bought at Dino's earlier in the afternoon. The store was crowded with last-minute Christmas shoppers, but the grotto had been closed, with a notice saying, *Sorry—gone back to North Pole for finishing touches. Will be back Christmas morning. Santa C.* Dino had even offered to sell the boys some of the gnomes, "dirt cheap," but Buzz and Wacko had declined, saying the three Wise Men were more seasonal.

The biggest difficulty arose over the most important item: the spotlight. The people at the photography store that rented out such equipment were sorry—the spotlights had all gone. There were plenty of bulbs, of course, of various colors and strengths. Wacko looked dismayed. "But without a spotlight the whole plan will be ruined!" Then Buzz remembered something.

So they ended their expedition back at Dino's, and Dino had been only too glad to sublease them the spotlight that had once lit up the last sentinel fairy.

It was now blazing down on the tree from the opposite far corner, behind Wacko's bed—a beam of strong white light that ended in an explosion of color with the streaming tinsel, the glass baubles and the three Wise Men.

Mrs. Williams was impressed when she looked in, just after 5:30.

"Well! I've never seen your room looking so—" Words failed her. "Well!"

"I thought we might as well brighten it up for the holiday, Mom."

"Sure! But—what's wrong with the tree downstairs?"

"Nothing, Mom. But—well—with having houseguests and all . . ."

"Of course!" said Mrs. Williams, smiling at Buzz. "Is everything OK, Robert?"

"Fine!" said Buzz. "Just fine!"

But he wondered what Mrs. Williams would have said if she'd picked up on Wacko's slip of the tongue and realized there were more than just the one houseguest present. With several more scheduled for later.

"Well, fellas," said Wacko, when his mother had gone downstairs, "d'you think it'll work?"

Carlos had been slowly pacing, studying the beam at every step. He now went to the word processor.

"It should work," he transmitted. *"With one or two minor adjustments, maybe."*

"Are you sure about the bulb now?" Wacko asked.

"Sure. As sure as I ever will be, anyway."

"Let's hope you're right," said Karen.

"Yeah!" said Danny, looking nervous.

"It seems OK to me," murmured Joe, studying the beam with narrowed eyes.

"How about your part of the plan, Joe?" Carlos asked. "Are you sure you'll be able to swing it with Purcell?"

"I'll give it my best shot," said Joe. "It may take a day or two, though. I don't want him to get too suspicious."

Carlos—the one who was always rushing into things—couldn't have agreed more.

"Naturally," he said. "Take all the time you need, Joe. Just know that *we're* ready." He turned. "And you, Danny. Are you sure you won't lose your nerve? When the crunch comes?"

Danny gulped.

"Nervous—I—I may be. But lose my nerve—no. No way!"

"Good," said Carlos, quietly.

Despite his own eagerness, Joe kept his head the following morning when he went to Hawkins Station and reported no progress so far in the Hermits' plan.

"You stayed all night?" Purcell asked, watching Joe's face.

"Sure!"

"How did he sleep?"

"Uneasy at first," said Joe. "Then deeper toward dawn."

"And no sign of any astral dream tendencies?"

"No," Joe said. "But it's early yet, I guess. Maybe tonight, when he's more used to sleeping in a strange bed—"

"Yes, well, I trust you'll be sure not to allow your attention to stray, Joseph?"

Joe wasn't quite sure how to take this. There seemed to be an irony underlining Purcell's words. But he kept up a show of enthusiasm.

"You bet, sir!"

The next morning was the tricky one.

Joe opened his report hesitantly.

"I—I have some bad news, sir."

"Oh?"

Purcell drawled the word, but his glittering eyes were fixed on Joe's—like needle points, ready to jab.

Muscle, Memory and Mermaid looked at Purcell expectantly—then at Joe.

"Yes." Joe shook his head. "Phillips might not be having those dreams nowadays."

"Really?"

This time the irony in Purcell's voice was much more apparent. Even Memory was indulging in a grim smile. Muscle stepped a couple of paces nearer. Mermaid, who'd been posing in the shaft of light, moved closer to the stage, a cruel gleam in her birdlike eyes.

"Yes, sir," said Joe, noting all this. "Maybe he only had them earlier in the year, when he was recovering from the shock of Green's death. I heard Phillips telling Williams about it last night."

Purcell's eyes had gone very narrow again.

"Memory?" he murmured.

"It could be the case, sir," sighed the gray ghost. "So far, I have gleaned no evidence from the records one way or the other."

"But the good news," Joe continued, with a more enthusiastic expression, "is that—"

"*Good* news?" said Purcell.

"Well, *I* think it might be, sir. I mean—"

"Huh!" grunted Muscle, looking very scornful.

"Be quiet!" snapped Purcell. "Go on, Joseph."

"The good news is that we might be able to get Phillips in another way."

Every pucker and wrinkle writhed as Purcell raised his eyebrows.

"And how do you propose we do that?"

"By *scaring* him out of his wits, sir! That's another way of detaching an astral body from the physical one. Like when someone gets mad, or drunk, or—"

"I know all the various modes, thank you," Purcell said coldly. "But *scaring* him? It is possible, of course, but it would have to be a very severe fright."

Joe faked an eager laugh.

"*You're* the only one who could do it, sir, but—"

"*I?*"

"Yes, sir. By making Green appear. The way you can make Mermaid appear. Phillips has gotten a terribly guilty conscience, remember—because of how Green died. So if Green suddenly showed up—" Then Joe let his shoulders slump. "But—well—maybe you couldn't do it, after all."

Purcell stiffened.

"Given the right circumstances, I could. But"—he glanced at the shaft of light and frowned—"it would mean luring him here. At exactly the right time on exactly the right kind of day. How do you propose to do *that?*"

Muscle leered. "Yeah! How?"

Joe ignored him. Still looking at Purcell, he said, "Well—sure—that *would* be difficult. But I thought I heard Memory once mention an experiment with a spotlight, at the Lakeview Hotel?"

Purcell shrugged.

"Yes. True. But—"

"Well, *they* have a spotlight. In Williams's room. Part of the Christmas decorations. Beamed onto a tree. And—well—I couldn't help thinking how similar it was to that shaft of sunlight there. As it was last Saturday. Same brightness, same—"

"White light?" said Purcell. "Not a *colored* light?"

"No, sir. White. Well—maybe slightly bluish white."

"Memory?" snapped Purcell.

"It's worth looking into, sir," said Memory, sounding much less vague. "But it means we should have to visit the place. You and I and, of course, Muscle."

"And why not?" said Purcell. "I like the idea! I like it! Joseph—this light may well turn out to be the wrong intensity, beamed at the wrong angle. These things have to be exactly right. But—as Memory says—it's worth pursuing further. Have you mentioned this to Green?"

"Yes, sir. He likes the idea, too. He's raring to—"

"You say this is part of the Christmas decorations?"

"Yes, sir. It'll probably be staying there for another week or so. But Phillips is only there for the next three days. And I thought that with this being Christmas Eve and visitors coming in and going out of the house, it would be a cinch for three or four of us to get in too."

Joe didn't have to hold his breath. Purcell's eyes were actually sparkling!

"The sooner the better!" he said. "And Christmas Eve! What a splendid time! What a splendid, splendid present for the Williams family! Heh! Their son's slayer! Gift-wrapped, too! Gift-wrapped in Phillips's body!"

19
Spotlight on Death

Around 7:30 that evening, Buzz and Wacko were sitting at the table, busy wrapping, or rewrapping, Wacko's presents for the rest of his family. The spaces they had cleared earlier were now littered with brightly colored paper, ribbons, rosettes and reels of Scotch tape. The chore was a good excuse for being up there for an hour or two when the rest of the family were partying downstairs.

The door was wide open, and they could hear the sounds of laughter and conversation from down below. Wacko's newly married sister and her husband were there, and other friends and neighbors kept coming and going. Buzz sighed as he struggled to replace in its original creases the wrapping on an electric shaver.

Wacko was muttering at the cussedness of a yellow rosette that had begun to unravel.

"I guess I'm all fingers and thumbs tonight!" he groaned.

"Is there any wonder?" murmured Buzz. "Considering—"

"Yeah, well," Wacko interrupted, giving him a warning frown, "I'm sorry! I know you're itching to go down and join the others, but I just couldn't rest until I'd checked these things out. Last year I presented Mom with a china cat, gift-wrapped at the store, that turned out to have a piece of its tail missing."

Buzz nodded. He knew whose ears these details were intended for. But he was afraid that his friend might be overdoing it.

"That's OK, Wacko. It's just that Christmas gets me like this. All charged up."

He went to the window, passing the brightly lit tree on his way.

"Listen! Carolers!" he said, peering out.

Unlike the "poor man" the people out there were singing about, they themselves had not yet come in sight.

"It's snowing again," Buzz said, watching the sleet slant down through the light from the window.

Somehow it reminded him of the need for absolute precision that Carlos and Wacko had talked about, the effect of light and filters, and all the other scientific stuff he just hadn't even begun to understand.

Was this *really* going to work?

He went back to the table and began to fumble with

a length of red ribbon that kept getting twisted when he attempted to tie a bow. He wondered, as he heard the door bell ring yet again, if *their* visitors had arrived yet—his and Wacko's.

His eyes strayed to the screen. It was dead. The word processor hadn't even been switched on. Nor would there be any using of the Ear Code.

"There will be a strict communications blackout," Carlos had warned. *"Joe and Danny can't risk so much as a touch, not even in the reddest of red alert situations, while Purcell and the others are in here."*

Buzz sighed again. It was terribly hard to bear, the lack of contact, when you knew how much there was at stake. He forced himself to think of the previous Christmas and how Danny had looked then, while still alive. He wondered if he really would be seeing Danny that evening. He knew, from what he and Wacko had been told over the word processor, just what Danny would be wearing. The same windbreaker and scarf he'd had on that last Christmas Eve. They'd been brand-new then, Christmas presents themselves. In fact they'd still been in good shape when the accident had happened, a few weeks later.

Buzz frowned.

If Danny did appear—how would he, Buzz Phillips, be affected?

He glanced over his shoulder. The beam of light was still shining unimpeded on the glittering tree. As he turned away, he noticed that Wacko's eyes were also straying in that direction. Well, it *was* difficult to keep from doing it.

"Do you think we put *too* much tinsel on the tree?" he said, trying to sound casual and hoping to justify their glances if Purcell and his stooges *should* be there.

"No—it's just fine," muttered Wacko, turning back to his wrapping paper.

Wacko appeared to be as tense as Buzz felt.

Had something gone wrong?

If Joe and Danny had come in with Purcell and the others already, how were things going?

Had Karen and Carlos managed to remain hidden and undetected in the closet, next to the spotlight stand?

Had Carlos been given easy enough access through the closet's half-open door? Easy enough for slipping out as quickly as was necessary to his plan? Would Purcell run a check for such hiding places?

All at once, Buzz found it desperately hard to keep his eyes from straying in *that* direction.

He began to hum an accompaniment to the carol that was now being sung somewhere outside.

> "Fear not," said he, for mighty dread
> Had seized their troubled mind. . . .

Had Joe and Carlos been right when they'd said that the Hermits would be too busy examining the beam?

> Thus spake the seraph, and forthwith
> Appeared a shining throng. . . .

Buzz found he was sweating slightly.

I mean, how *will* I take it? he asked himself. If—when—*if* Danny does appear?

Now that the possibility was imminent, he wasn't

sure. Of course, if the ghost of Danny had ever appeared suddenly, without warning, he, Buzz Phillips, *would* have been scared out of his wits. No doubt about that! But being prepared for it was worse, in a way. He'd been bracing himself so tight that every muscle in his body seemed to ache. No wonder he—

There'd been a sudden change of light. Very subtle. Very slight. But very definite.

He turned and glanced at the beam—then froze.

"Danny!" he gasped.

For it was happening! His dead friend was appearing! First the head . . . then the scarf . . . then the shoulders. And yes—now the whole of the body down to the waist, every crease in the shiny black windbreaker looking as real as it had before the accident!

And Danny's face was the same, too—still pale and peaky, with the eyes looking large as they rested on Buzz, glowing. Then the mouth began to move, seeming to form the words *Hi, Buzz!*—but almost at once the whole face began to blur, and when it cleared, the mouth was closed again, and Danny's expression had frozen.

"Can—can you—?"

Buzz's whisper broke off as the face of his dead friend turned quickly, and the eyes became anxious. Then Danny's body, which by this time had become visible down to the knees, slipped sideways, out of the beam, disappearing as it did so.

"What—?"

"Quiet, Buzz!" came Wacko's murmur.

"But—did *you* see it?"

197

"I saw it," said Wacko, in a low trembling voice.

They didn't return to their gift wrapping. They knew that all hell was probably breaking loose in that room now—even though nothing was disturbed. No furniture was overturned. Not a single ornament was knocked off the tree. Not even a strand of tinsel had been made to stir. And no shadow that *they* could see crossed that beam of light.

And there were no sounds, either, other than the genial hubbub of conversation from down below and the singing of the carolers, now very close.

> Silent night, holy night.
> All is calm, all is bright. . . .

It was hard to imagine that right then, in that same peaceful room, the fates of the Ghost Squad and the Prowling Hermits were being settled and sealed. . . .

The ghost visitors had experienced no difficulty getting into the house. Besides Joe and Danny, there were only Purcell, Memory and Muscle, and it was easy for the five of them to slip by through the open door while a couple of living visitors exchanged greetings with Mr. Williams and paused on the doorstep to kick the caked snow from their boots. In fact, there would have been time for at least one more to enter, but Mermaid had been told to stay outside with Flowery Shirt, much to her disgust.

As soon as Purcell and the other two Hermits entered Wacko's room, they looked around curiously.

Purcell and Muscle were more concerned at first with observing Buzz and Wacko.

"You didn't tell me there was a party downstairs," Purcell said to Joe, seemingly casually, as he continued his scrutiny of the two boys.

"I just didn't know about it," said Joe.

"It seems strange that these two should not be downstairs, enjoying themselves with the rest," said Purcell.

"Oh—yeah—sure," said Joe. "And I guess they will, when they're through wrapping the gifts. But—"

Just then, Wacko made the remark to Buzz about needing to be sure that none of the gifts was damaged.

Joe breathed easier. Wacko's comment couldn't have been better timed. Purcell seemed satisfied. He turned to study the beam of light.

"What do you think, Memory?"

Memory had been holding his frail hand in the beam, studying it closely.

"Frankly I am amazed!" he said. "Astonished!"

"Oh?" Purcell's voice had an ominously sharp note. "Why? What's wrong?"

At that point, Buzz had gone to the window to look out for the carolers, but none of the ghosts paid him any attention now.

"Wrong, sir?" said Memory, looking up along the beam to its source, then down its widening path to the glittering, flashing tree. "*Wrong?* . . . Why, nothing! Absolutely nothing! It's perfect!"

Purcell's mouth twitched wider in one of his rare smiles. He turned.

"Well done, Joseph! Your instincts were right, after all." Then—as Buzz went back to his seat—Purcell brought the palms of both hands together with a dull leathery clap. "But now—to work! Green—go stand in front of the tree, facing Phillips."

Danny, looking very tense, did as he'd been told.

Memory went up to him, gazed up the beam, then at Buzz and Wacko, then at Danny.

"Just another inch backward," he murmured. "No! Too far. Forward a hairsbreadth. There! Stay just so."

Danny gave Joe a quick imploring look. Joe pretended not to see it. He didn't want the squad's key member having stage fright *now!*

"Look at *Phillips!*" barked Purcell. "Not at Joseph, you fool!"

Joe glanced at Purcell. Every pucker and wrinkle seemed to have set hard, immobile, never to stir again—so tense was *he* now.

Memory said softly, "When Dr. Purcell makes you appear, you should simply be staring at Phillips—accusingly. That should be more than sufficient to give him the shock of his life."

"Yes, sir," whispered Danny. "I—"

"And don't—repeat do *not*—try to speak to him," said Memory. "Even though he will be seeing you, he will not be able to hear you."

"And the movement of your lips," added Purcell, "will tend to make you, or that part of you, disappear from the subject's sight. *Any* movement will."

Danny gulped.

200

"OK?" growled Joe. "You heard what Dr. Purcell said? Stand perfectly still!"

"S-sure! I—"

"Silence!" Joe snapped.

Purcell looked at him approvingly.

"As for you, Joseph, there's hardly any need to remind *you*, I know. But you will stand close to Phillips the whole time, ready to take over. And don't forget—the astral body should be at least three paces from the parent body before you make your move."

"Yes, sir," said Joe. "But I've been thinking—supposing the astral body doesn't go that far?"

"It will!" drawled Muscle. "If I have to drag it away, it'll move that f-far!"

He was glaring at Buzz.

"Quite so," said Purcell. "And this one, when it *is* far enough away, you may kill."

Joe felt a tremor of fear. Suppose something went wrong? What if Carlos had made a faulty calculation?

But it was too late to unscramble everything now.

"All set?" Purcell asked.

"All set, sir," echoed Memory.

Purcell moved into the beam, a couple of yards away from Danny.

"Not quite so close, sir. Step back a little."

"Is this better?" murmured Purcell, stepping back but keeping his head bent slightly forward, the unblinking lizard eyes fixed on Danny.

"Perfect, sir! Your shadow is now providing optimum coverage."

The faint dullness of Purcell's shadow had cast a kind of film over the whole of Danny's figure. It was difficult for Joe to realize that the shadow Danny himself had been casting on the tree hadn't been visible to the eyes of the living, but just then, reminding Joe of the great difference, Buzz turned to the riot of color and said, "Do you think we put *too* much tinsel on the tree?"

None of the others paid this any attention. Muscle and Memory were staring first at Purcell, then at Danny.

"Look toward Phillips, not at me!" said Purcell.

Danny quickly obeyed.

Purcell's eyes began to narrow to slits, then dwindled to tiny glittering points.

Somewhere outside, the carolers had struck up with "While Shepherds Watched Their Flocks by Night."

Joe—like Buzz at that very moment—fought to keep himself from glancing at the open closet door.

Purcell's shadow had started to vibrate, just as it had done when eclipsing Mermaid's body at Hawkins Station.

And now—yes—it was Danny's body that seemed to light up, starting with the head, then the shoulders.

"Danny!" Buzz gasped.

Danny's body was now lit up as far down as the waist. Purcell himself seemed to be finely trembling as he crouched there, concentrating.

But now Danny's mouth was moving.

"Hi, Buzz!"

"Keep still!" hissed Memory.

202

For a few seconds, a hole seemed to appear in Purcell's strangely bright shadow, just over the lower half of Danny's face. Danny closed his mouth, and the brightness was restored.

"Can—can you—?" Buzz began.

Which was when Carlos slipped out of the closet and into the beam close to the spotlight stand, casting an immediate shadow—a true dull filmy shadow— over Purcell.

Purcell gave a sharp cry and swung around.

Danny turned, saw Carlos, and sidestepped out of the beam.

Purcell was staring at Carlos, the reptile face contorted with surprise, outrage, fury. He seemed to have become paralyzed, incapable of moving either toward Carlos or out of the beam. He was fixed there, still crouched, half-turned toward Carlos, arms slightly raised and hooked, ready to grapple, crablike.

But there was something else, too.

Joe's eyes popped. Purcell seemed to be—correction, *was*—beginning to fade!

Muscle gave a startled grunt and began to move toward Carlos. But before Joe could block Muscle's advance, Memory's voice cut through.

"Stay where you are, Muscle! One hasty move, and you could destroy Dr. Purcell!"

The bodyguard stopped in his tracks. Every muscle in his face and neck seemed to twitch as the black glasses turned to Memory, then to Purcell.

Purcell's trembling had become coarser, more violent, even as the fading progressed.

203

"Memory," he croaked—but even the croak was fading, "*do* something. . . ."

"Of course, sir!" Memory's voice was no longer a weak echo of Purcell's. It seemed sharper, crisper, more confident. "Stay quite still."

Joe watched, ready for any sudden movement Memory might make. But the gray ghost was standing perfectly still himself, gazing at Carlos with an odd light in his eyes.

Carlos was watching Purcell with eyes as narrow as Purcell's had been. Carlos's stance was similar, too—a forward-tending crouch, almost as if he were preparing to pounce.

"Memory—I—I . . ."

Purcell's words were like the faint rattle of dead leaves being blown across a tombstone at midnight. His figure had faded to a shadow.

"Good-bye, Dr. Purcell!" Memory spoke softly and pleasantly, but with a cruel smile. "I think you have met your match at last!"

There was a sudden shiver of light, a bright shimmering, where Purcell had been standing.

Then nothing. Not even a blur.

The spotlight shone freely on the tree as Carlos stepped out of the beam and joined Karen, who'd crept out of the closet unnoticed.

Muscle stared at the spot where he'd last seen his leader.

"What—what's happened?" he said, in an awed whisper.

Memory ignored him. He was busy addressing Carlos.

"Congratulations, sir! I knew you were a genius, of *course!* But this—" Memory shook his head. "To be able to boost the second-state energy to such a level and maintain it for that length of time—" His eyes were shining. "Muscle, I think we have found a new leader, far more clever and more potent than Purcell ever—"

"*Him?*" Muscle blurted, turning to Carlos.

"*Me?*" blurted Carlos, almost simultaneously.

Carlos was looking more like his usual self. There had been a big grin on his face, and his eyes were dancing before Memory had begun that announcement.

"Yes, sir," said Memory. "With the facilities I'm able to make available to you, not least a memory as reliable as any computer's—well! Imagine the power you will have! Why, we may even devise a means of communicating directly with your friends here." He glanced at Buzz and Wacko, still sitting there, stunned by Danny's brief manifestation. "We—"

"Oh, yeah?" said Carlos, his eyes suddenly flashing. "What do *you* care about my friends? You came here tonight hoping to take one of them over and then kill the other!"

Memory looked pained.

"*He* came here for that purpose, sir. Purcell. Not *we.* We just did as he told us—which was becoming more and more the wrong thing, the ultimately stupid thing. Isn't that right, Muscle? Hadn't we *all* started to realize the doctor's limitations?"

Muscle looked dazed.

"Uh—well—yeah . . . I guess."

"Of *course* we did!" said Memory. "But now we've found a more powerful, an infinitely more skillful manipulator in Mr. Gomez. Someone who could really help us achieve our ambitions and—"

That was when Joe stepped in.

"I think Mr. Gomez would like some time to discuss the matter with his *real* friends, his *first* followers."

Memory flashed Joe a hostile look, but Carlos said, "Yes, I *would!* Thank you—uh—Joseph."

Memory bowed.

"Of course, sir!" He turned to Joe and said, less warmly but with respect, "I presume you were sent by Mr. Gomez to take the true measure of Purcell?"

"I—yeah—I was. It was kind of scary, going undercover among you guys—but what Mr. Gomez wants you to do, you do."

"Naturally!" said Memory.

"And what I want now," said Carlos, putting on a stern expression, "is for you and you"—he nodded at Memory and Muscle—"to get out of here. I'll let you know when I'm ready to talk."

Outside the house, the carolers were striking up with "Hark! The Herald Angels Sing."

"Certainly, sir," said Memory. "You must be very tired, mentally."

"Yeah," grunted Muscle, completely awed.

"Some," said Carlos, shrugging and stifling a yawn.

"Joseph—Mr. Williams will shortly be opening the door downstairs to thank the singers. Kindly show our—uh—guests out. They have some pretty important news to break to the rest of their bunch!"

20
Ghosts for Christmas

When Joe came back, after making sure that Memory and Muscle had left the house, he found the other ghosts at the window. Karen turned, smiling.

"Did you see Mermaid and Flowery Shirt?" she said. "When Memory and Muscle went across to them?"

"Not with all the carolers still blocking my view," said Joe. "Why? How did Mermaid take it?"

"I thought she was going to faint," said Danny.

"Flowery Shirt didn't seem so cool, either," said Carlos. "Especially when he looked up here, and I ordered them off." He made an imperious, dismissive gesture. "Begone, dogs!" Carlos laughed. "They went, of course. When Gomez says *go*, they go. Right, Joseph?"

"OK," said Joe. "You can cut that out now—*Dr. Gomez!*"

"Yes, sir, Mr. Armstrong, sir! Sorry, sir!" said Carlos, pretending to cower.

Wacko and Buzz were still sitting stunned.

"You—you really did see it, Wacko?" murmured Buzz. "I mean you're not just *saying* so?"

Wacko shook his head.

"It wasn't your imagination playing tricks, if that's what you're worried about. Sure I saw it!"

"And you recognized it—him?"

"It was Danny, all right. Yeah."

They were still speaking guardedly, not knowing who might be listening.

"Let's put them out of their suspense, huh?" said Joe, touching Buzz's right ear.

Carlos did the same to Wacko's right ear.

Buzz and Wacko looked at each other.

Again they were given the yes signal.

"Is—everything OK?" Wacko ventured.

Yes, yes, yes, yes, *yes*. . . .

"Terrific!" said Wacko, switching on the word processor.

Three pairs of ghost eyes watched Carlos as he took up his stance in front of the keyboard. Was it asking too much, after such a strenuous performance? He did seem somewhat reluctant, unsure of himself. . . .

But they had forgotten one thing.

Carlos's love of high drama.

With a sly glance over his shoulder at the three

worried faces, he suddenly laughed—and the next moment his fingers were dancing as nimbly as ever.

"Merry Christmas, you guys!" The words came flickering across the screen. *"We did it, we did it, we did it!!!"*

For the next half hour, the word processor was busy as Carlos transmitted the details of their victory. When he was through, Buzz sighed.

"And you're sure that *was* the end of Purcell?"

"Positive! Absolutely certain! Wherever Maggot is now, Purcell will have gone to join him!"

"How about Memory?" Wacko asked.

Joe dictated the answer.

"He won't give us any trouble. He's too much in awe of Carlos. He'll wait patiently for a while, hoping that Carlos will be in touch. [Which I won't be! C.G.] But the others won't be so patient. They'll soon start turning against each other, now that they've lost their leader. Muscle will blame Memory for not lifting a finger to save Purcell. Mermaid will blame both Memory and Muscle. And like that. Everyone blaming everyone else. Come New Year's, they'll either have torn each other to shreds or they'll all have scattered— going back to being just ordinary individual Malevs. Nuisances but no major threat."

"So we did ourselves a favor!" said Buzz, looking very relieved.

"So we did everyone a favor, everyone, everywhere— ghosts and living alike. Purcell was bad news, believe me!"

"What's all this?"

Six heads turned sharply. None of the squad had heard Mrs. Williams approach the open door.

210

She was staring at the screen.

"Ghosts? Purcell?" she said. "Is that the Dr. Purcell your father—?"

"Yes, Mom," said Wacko, hurriedly switching off the machine. "We—we were just trying our hand at a ghost story. We thought it might be fun to tell it later, at the party."

"Kind of a personalized ghost story," said Buzz.

"Yeah!" said Wacko. "About how Dr. Purcell comes back as a ghost and tries to avenge himself on our family by—"

"Hey! Stop!" said Mrs. Williams. "That's getting *too* close to home! . . . Anyway, I came up to see if you're ready to join us. As a matter of fact, we're about to have a *real* ghost-story session, around the fire."

"Huh?"

Wacko looked startled.

"Yes," his mother said. "Mr. Burchardt has brought along a new videotape. *Ghosts for Christmas* it's called. Something like that. It features the actor who's been performing at Carmen's Cookery over the past few days."

"Franklin Winterbourne?" said Buzz.

"That's the guy," said Mrs. Williams.

"Hey!" said Wacko. "Now he *really* knows how to tell ghost stories!"

"Yeah!" said Buzz. "They say he actually *met* a ghost once."

"That's right," said Wacko. "In the shape of Santa Claus."

"So why don't you both come down?" said Mrs. Williams. "You might pick up some pointers."

Buzz and Wacko hesitated, obviously reluctant to break up the session with their partners.

Joe grinned at the others.

"Why not?" he said.

"I guess we could use a little relaxation," said Danny.

"I think we *deserve* it!" said Karen.

"You can say *that* again!" said Carlos.

Both of their living colleagues then felt a tattoo of touches on their right ears.

"You bet!" said Buzz, following Mrs. Williams.

"Sure!" said Wacko, taking care to leave the door wide open.